The Shattered Queen

A World on the Brink, a Leader Unwilling, a Destiny Unraveled

J.A. Thornhill

Copyright © 2024 by J.A. Thornhill

All rights reserved. No part of this book may be used or reproduced in any form whatsoever without written permission except in the case of brief quotations in critical articles or reviews.

First Edition: November 2024

Table of Contents

Chapter 1 The Relic's Whisper 1

Chapter 2 Through the Rift 17

Chapter 3 Among Strangers 35

Chapter 4 The Mark of Seluna 52

Chapter 5 Trials in the Jungle 68

Chapter 6 Shadows in the Wild 85

Chapter 7 Fractured Memories 103

Chapter 8 Secrets of the Past 120

Chapter 9 The First Fragment 137

Chapter 10 Bonds Forged in Strife 155

Chapter 11 The Rift's Reach 173

Chapter 12 Divided Hearts 189

Chapter 13 The Weight of Leadership 205

Chapter 14 The Shard of Light 222

Chapter 15 Threads of Unity 238

Epilogue A World Rebuilt 254

Chapter 1
The Relic's Whisper

The Temple of Seluna was a marvel of ancient craftsmanship, even in its ruined state. Shafts of sunlight pierced through cracks in the stone ceiling, casting long shadows across the intricate mosaics on the floor. Dust motes floated lazily in the still air, adding an ethereal quality to the space. Aria Valen paused mid-step, her breath catching as her gaze swept over the towering stone walls. Intricate carvings—vines interwoven with celestial patterns and figures that seemed almost alive—adorned every surface.

"This is incredible," she murmured, her voice reverent in the vast emptiness.

The sound of her boots crunching softly against the broken tiles echoed faintly. She adjusted the strap of her pack and stepped closer to one of the walls, her fingers hovering just above the carvings. The historian in her thrummed with excitement. The carvings were unlike anything she had studied before—alien, yet undeniably purposeful.

"Not in any of the texts," she muttered, pulling out her notebook. Her pen scratched against the paper as she quickly sketched the details. "Whoever built this… they were masterful."

Her voice, though quiet, seemed loud in the silence of the chamber. Aria glanced over her shoulder, half expecting someone—or something—to respond. But there was only the faint sound of her breathing. She exhaled sharply, shaking her head.

"Don't let it get to you, Valen," she told herself. "It's just a temple."

Still, she couldn't shake the feeling that the air itself was alive with anticipation.

Her flashlight flickered as she moved deeper into the chamber. At the center of the room stood a pedestal, and atop it rested an object that seemed untouched by the decay around it. The relic was a circular artifact, gleaming with a silvery light that shifted as if it were liquid. Its surface reflected the room in perfect detail, yet her own image was absent from its mirrored sheen.

"What the…?" Aria whispered, stepping closer.

She reached out instinctively, but her hand hesitated just above the relic. A strange hum vibrated in the air, faint but persistent. She felt it in her fingertips, a pulse that seemed to match the rhythm of her own heartbeat.

"Is it… alive?" she wondered aloud.

Her rational mind screamed at her to stop. She'd read too many accounts of ancient artifacts with dire consequences. But curiosity gnawed at her—a historian's curse. This relic was more than a piece of history. It was a key to understanding the unknown.

"I shouldn't," she muttered, her voice barely audible.

Yet, as if in answer, the relic began to emit a faint whisper. The sound was indistinct at first, like the rustle of leaves in the wind. But then it became clearer, forming syllables in a language she didn't recognize. Her name—Aria—emerged, spoken in a tone both gentle and commanding.

Her eyes widened. "What the hell?"

She took a step back, heart pounding. "No, no, no. That's not possible. It's a trick."

But there was no denying what she had heard. The whisper came again, this time louder, insistent. The hum in the air intensified, and the light from the relic grew brighter. Aria's breathing quickened as a strange pull gripped her—a force that wasn't entirely physical.

"Alright," she said shakily. "If this kills me, at least they'll know I died doing what I love."

She reached out again, her hand trembling. The hum surged as her fingers brushed the surface of the relic. It was warm, almost alive. The whisper became a chorus, a symphony of alien voices that resonated deep within her.

"What is this?" she whispered, her voice barely audible.

The relic pulsed with energy, sending a jolt up her arm. Aria gasped, stumbling back, but her gaze remained locked on the artifact. The pull was stronger now, irresistible. It wasn't just calling to her—it was beckoning her forward, drawing her into its enigmatic embrace.

"Okay," she said, her voice a mix of fear and determination. "You've got my attention."

Her hand hovered once more over the relic. This time, she didn't hesitate. She pressed her palm flat against its surface, and the world around her shifted. The air crackled, the chamber dissolving into a cascade of light and sound. Aria cried out, but the sound was swallowed by the rising storm of energy.

Then, as suddenly as it began, everything fell silent. The whispering ceased, the hum dissipated, and the chamber grew still once more. Aria stumbled back, her knees buckling, but she caught herself on the edge of the pedestal.

She stared at the relic, her heart racing. It no longer glowed, its surface now a dull, lifeless gray. But the memory of its warmth lingered in her palm, and the echo of the whispers reverberated in her mind.

"What just happened?" she whispered.

The silence offered no answer. But deep down, Aria knew—this was only the beginning.

The moment Aria's hand met the relic's smooth surface, the glow intensified, swallowing the chamber in a blinding silvery light. She gasped as the heat from the object surged through her palm, radiating up her arm and spreading through her body. The whispers returned, louder and more insistent, their alien syllables overlapping in a haunting melody that seemed to come from everywhere and nowhere.

"What is this?" she cried, trying to pull her hand away.

But it was too late. The relic held her fast, its warmth turning to an almost unbearable heat. The hum in the air grew to a deafening roar, and the chamber around her began to distort. The carvings on the walls shimmered and twisted, their celestial figures writhing as though coming alive.

"No, no, no!" Aria yelled, panic rising in her chest. "This isn't happening!"

A rush of wind exploded outward from the relic, sending her hair whipping around her face and scattering dust and debris across the chamber. The world began to fracture—shards of light splitting from the edges of her vision and bleeding into the air. Her body felt weightless, as though she were being pulled from reality itself.

"Let go!" she screamed, pulling with all her strength, but her hand remained glued to the relic.

The whispers became a cacophony, each voice layering over the next in a sound that was both beautiful and horrifying. The wind roared louder, carrying with it faint echoes of a distant world—birds calling, leaves rustling, water rushing over rocks. These sounds felt closer than the chamber itself, as though the temple were fading away.

Her legs gave out beneath her, but she didn't fall. Instead, the pull from the relic lifted her, suspending her in midair. The light grew brighter still, until she could see nothing else, her entire world reduced to shimmering silver and piercing sound.

And then, just as suddenly, there was silence.

The roar ceased. The whispers stopped. The light dimmed to nothingness, leaving behind only a deep, inky black. Aria felt the ground beneath her feet again, solid but unfamiliar. Her breath came in sharp, ragged gasps as she tried to orient herself. The weightlessness was gone, replaced by an oppressive heaviness in the air.

She blinked, her eyes adjusting to the faint glow of her flashlight, which lay flickering weakly a few feet away. Slowly, she reached for it, her fingers trembling as they brushed the cold metal.

"What… where…" Her voice cracked, barely audible in the dense silence.

She lifted the flashlight, its beam cutting through a thick mist that clung to the ground. Massive trees loomed around her, their trunks twisted and ancient. Their gnarled roots clawed at the damp earth, and their leaves shimmered faintly, catching the weak light in strange, iridescent hues.

"This isn't possible," she muttered, shaking her head. "The temple… I was just…"

She turned in a slow circle, her heart pounding. The chamber of the Temple of Seluna was gone, replaced by a sprawling, alien jungle that stretched into shadowed infinity. The air was heavy with moisture, carrying the sharp scent of earth and foliage, mingled with something sweet and unfamiliar.

"Okay, Aria," she whispered to herself, her voice trembling. "Think. You touched the relic. It… did something. But this? This can't be real."

Her legs felt unsteady as she took a tentative step forward, the thick underbrush crunching beneath her boots. The beam of her flashlight illuminated swirls of mist, but it did little to pierce the gloom beyond. Every shadow seemed alive, shifting as though it were watching her.

The ground beneath her foot squelched, and she stumbled slightly, catching herself against a tree trunk. Its bark was rough and oddly warm, sending a shiver up her spine. She pulled her hand away quickly, as though burned.

"Where am I?" she whispered, her voice barely audible.

A faint sound reached her ears—rustling leaves, distant but deliberate. She froze, her breath catching in her throat. The sound grew closer, accompanied by something more—soft, rhythmic voices murmuring words she couldn't understand. They were melodic, almost musical, but laced with a sharp, alien edge.

"Hello?" she called out, her voice shaking. "Is someone there?"

The voices stopped. The silence that followed was suffocating.

Aria gripped the flashlight tighter, its weak beam wavering as her hands trembled. She took another step forward, her ears straining for any hint of movement. Her heart hammered against her ribs, the sound deafening in the oppressive quiet.

"Calm down," she muttered to herself, forcing her breaths to slow. "You're a historian. You figure things out. Just… just figure this out."

She crouched, her fingers brushing the damp ground. It felt real—too real for this to be some sort of hallucination. The smells, the sounds, the oppressive humidity—none of it felt like a dream.

"Okay," she said, louder this time, as though the words might anchor her. "If I'm not in the temple anymore… then where the hell am I?"

The mist swirled around her, and the shadows seemed to draw closer, as though answering her question.

For the first time, Aria felt truly, utterly alone.

The oppressive silence of the jungle stretched taut around Aria, her heartbeat the only sound she could hear over the faint rustle of leaves in the distance. She gripped the flashlight tightly, her knuckles white as she scanned the misty shadows around her.

Every shifting leaf or snapping twig sent a fresh wave of adrenaline coursing through her.

"Get a grip," she whispered to herself, though her voice was barely audible. "You've handled ruins, dark tombs, and creepy basements. This is just… another place."

Another place, yes—but one where the air felt alive with eyes watching her. Her flashlight flickered again, the beam dimming before sputtering back to life. She aimed it into the trees, the light catching brief flashes of movement—shadows slipping between the massive trunks.

"Hello?" she called, the word sticking in her throat. "Is anyone there?"

The foliage shifted with deliberate slowness, as if something—or someone—was circling her. A low murmur reached her ears, faint but rhythmic. It wasn't the chaotic noise of wild animals; it was deliberate, structured, a language she couldn't understand.

Her voice rose, shaky but forceful. "I'm not here to hurt anyone! I—I don't know where I am!"

No answer came, only the steady rustling of leaves and the whispers that seemed to draw closer. The beam of her flashlight caught the edge of a figure—a flash of painted skin and gleaming eyes—before it disappeared into the shadows again.

"I can see you!" she said, her panic betraying the confidence she tried to project. "If you're people… just come out. Please."

A branch snapped sharply to her left, and she whipped around, her light landing on a figure stepping into view. Aria's breath caught in her throat. The person—no, the warrior—stood tall and imposing, their face painted with intricate patterns of black and white that accentuated their sharp, piercing eyes. They carried a spear, its tip glinting faintly in the dim light, though it was pointed downward.

Aria stumbled back, raising her hands instinctively. "Wait—don't come any closer! I don't mean any harm!"

The warrior's gaze bore into her, their expression unreadable beneath the paint. Their lips moved, forming words she couldn't understand, their tone low and steady. They spoke again, the same word repeated like a mantra: "Seluna."

"What?" Aria said, blinking rapidly. "Seluna? Is that… the temple? The relic?"

The warrior tilted their head slightly, studying her with an intensity that made her skin crawl. More figures emerged from the mist, slipping silently from the shadows to encircle her. Each one was clad in primitive armor adorned with feathers, bone, and carved beads. Their faces bore similar painted patterns, and their weapons—spears, knives, and bows—gleamed faintly in the flickering light.

Aria turned in a slow circle, her hands still raised. "Okay, okay," she stammered, her voice trembling. "You're people, that's good. People are better than wild animals. We can talk, right? You can understand me?"

The warriors exchanged glances, their murmurs blending into a rhythmic hum. She caught the word again—"Seluna"—uttered with reverence and, perhaps, a hint of fear. Their movements were synchronized, their eyes darting between her and one another, as though trying to decide what to do.

Aria tried again. "Seluna. Yes, I came from there. The temple. The relic. Do you know about it?"

One of the warriors stepped forward—a man taller than the rest, with a scar cutting across his cheek and a necklace of claws hanging from his neck. He raised a hand, and the murmurs ceased instantly. His voice was deeper than the others', commanding but calm as he addressed her in their strange, musical language.

"I don't understand you," Aria said, shaking her head. "I don't… Seluna? What does that mean?"

The scarred warrior held her gaze for a moment before gesturing sharply to two of his companions. They moved swiftly, closing the circle tighter around her. Aria's pulse spiked, and she stepped back until her shoulders met the rough bark of a tree.

"Wait!" she exclaimed, her voice breaking. "You don't need to—"

Before she could finish, one of the warriors reached for her, their grip firm but not rough as they pulled her forward. Another produced a length of cloth, tying her wrists together with practiced ease. The scarred man barked another order, and the group began moving, tugging her along with them.

"Wait, please!" Aria struggled against the bindings, her words spilling out in a panicked rush. "I don't know what's happening! I'm not supposed to be here! Seluna—it's just a temple, right? It's—"

Her words faltered as the scarred warrior turned, silencing her with a single look. His eyes were dark and intense, filled with something she couldn't name—curiosity? Suspicion? Whatever it was, it wasn't cruelty. He said one word, slow and deliberate, as though trying to make her understand.

"Seluna."

Aria's breath caught in her throat. The way he said it—like a name, or a title—made her stomach twist. This wasn't just about the temple. To these people, "Seluna" meant something more. Something sacred.

They led her deeper into the jungle, the mist swallowing the strange group. Aria stumbled over roots and rocks, the bindings around her wrists cutting into her skin. The whispers among the warriors grew louder, more fervent, as faint lights began to flicker ahead.

A village. Aria's chest tightened as the reality of her situation sank in. Whatever "Seluna" meant, whatever they thought she was, one thing was clear: she wasn't going home anytime soon.

The jungle's oppressive silence seemed to close in around Aria as the warriors guided her forward, their movements deliberate and synchronized. Her hands, bound tightly with a cloth that bit into her skin, ached with each tug of the makeshift rope. The flashlight she had clung to earlier now dangled uselessly at her side, its faint beam swallowed by the mist that clung to the ground.

"Please," Aria began, her voice cracking as she stumbled over a root. "You don't understand. I'm not here to hurt anyone! I don't even know where I am!"

Her words fell into the void, met only by the rhythmic rustling of leaves underfoot and the soft murmur of the warriors' voices. They spoke to one another in their musical, alien language, their tones shifting between sharp commands and low, reverent whispers. Occasionally, the word "Seluna" surfaced, hanging in the air like a fragment of an unsolvable puzzle.

The tall warrior with the scar, clearly their leader, glanced back at her, his expression unreadable beneath the intricate paint on his face. When he spoke, his tone was steady, almost soothing, but the words were incomprehensible to her.

"Seluna," he said again, gesturing toward her as if to emphasize his point.

Aria shook her head desperately. "I don't know what that means! I don't—Seluna is just a temple! A name on a map! I don't belong here!"

The leader tilted his head slightly, as though considering her protests, but said nothing more. Instead, he barked an order to his companions, and they tightened their formation around her, their spears shifting slightly closer—not threatening, but undeniably firm.

Frustration bubbled to the surface, and Aria dug her heels into the damp earth. "Stop!" she snapped, her voice rising. "I'm not going anywhere until someone explains what's happening!"

Her resistance earned her nothing but an impatient tug from one of the warriors, pulling her forward with surprising gentleness. She stumbled, nearly losing her balance, and felt the heat rise in her cheeks as anger mixed with helplessness.

"This is insane," she muttered under her breath. "Completely insane."

The scarred leader turned again, his gaze lingering on her for a moment longer this time. He spoke a single word in his language, and the warrior beside her responded with a brief nod. Whatever was exchanged between them, it only deepened the knot in her stomach.

The jungle stretched on endlessly, its towering trees and dense mist distorting her sense of time. Her feet sank into the soft earth with each step, the terrain uneven and treacherous. The warriors moved effortlessly, their bare feet gliding over roots and stones as if they knew every inch of this place. Aria, in contrast, tripped and stumbled, her bound hands making it nearly impossible to steady herself.

She fell again, her knee slamming into a gnarled root. Pain shot up her leg, and she let out a hiss of frustration. "Can you just stop for one second?" she snapped, her voice shaking. "I'm not exactly built for… whatever this is!"

One of the warriors, a younger man with paint streaked across his cheeks, stepped forward and extended a hand to help her up. His grip was firm but not rough, and for a moment, his expression softened. Before she could say anything, the scarred leader barked another command, and the young warrior quickly released her, stepping back into formation.

Aria's breath came in short, ragged gasps as she pushed herself upright, her muscles burning with every step. Her mind raced as she tried to piece together what was happening. These people clearly thought she was connected to the relic—or to whatever "Seluna" meant—but why? What did they want from her?

"Look," she said, her voice quieter now, almost pleading. "I'm not who you think I am. I touched the relic, yes, but it doesn't mean anything. I don't know anything about your prophecy or your rituals or… whatever this is."

The leader didn't turn this time, his focus locked ahead as the jungle began to thin. Aria noticed the faint flicker of firelight in the distance, the unmistakable glow of torches cutting through the mist. Her stomach tightened as they drew closer, the reality of her situation sinking in.

The village came into view slowly, like a mirage forming in the fog. Dozens of huts made of woven leaves and wood stood clustered around a central clearing, where a massive bonfire burned brightly. Shadows danced across the faces of the villagers gathered there, their painted expressions somber and expectant. The hum of voices rose as the warriors approached, carrying her like an offering.

Aria's steps faltered, and she tried to pull back, but the young warrior at her side steadied her with a firm hand. "Please," she whispered, her voice barely audible. "Please, I'm not supposed to be here. You don't understand—I don't belong here."

The scarred leader turned one last time, his dark eyes meeting hers. For a moment, she thought she saw a flicker of something in his gaze—sympathy, perhaps, or hesitation. But it was gone as quickly as it came. He gestured toward the fire, and the warriors led her forward, the murmurs of the villagers growing louder.

As the heat of the flames washed over her, Aria felt a chill settle deep in her chest. This wasn't just a misunderstanding or a simple case of mistaken identity. Whatever these people believed, whatever they thought she was, it was bigger than her. Bigger than anything she could understand.

For the first time, the possibility hit her with full force. She might never find her way home.

Chapter 2
Through the Rift

The flickering light from the village's central fire danced across the walls of the structure where Aria had been left. She sat on a low wooden bench, her bound wrists resting on her knees, the rough rope biting into her skin. Her eyes darted around the room—a mix of curiosity and growing dread. The interior was spartan but purposeful. Carved symbols adorned the walls, and bundles of dried herbs hung from the ceiling, their faint, earthy scent mingling with the smoke from the torches outside.

The low murmur of voices filtered through the walls, but Aria couldn't make out the words. She leaned her head back against the cool wood, closing her eyes for a moment. "This isn't real," she whispered to herself. "It can't be real."

The sound of footsteps snapped her out of her thoughts. The heavy wooden door creaked open, and a figure stepped inside. He was tall, broad-shouldered, and cloaked in dark leather armor that bore the same swirling patterns she'd seen on the warriors. His face was sharp and angular, marked by a faint scar along his jawline. His expression was unreadable, his piercing eyes fixed on her as he shut the door behind him.

Aria sat up straighter, her pulse quickening. "Let me guess," she said, her voice edged with sarcasm. "You're here to tell me I'm some sort of prophecy?"

The man didn't respond immediately. Instead, he crossed the room with measured steps, stopping a few feet away. His arms were folded, and his gaze remained locked on hers.

"Do you speak my language?" Aria pressed, her voice rising slightly. "Because if you do, we're going to need to clear up a few things. First, I'm not your queen, or chosen one, or whatever—"

"You talk too much," the man said abruptly, his voice low and gravelly. His accent was thick, but his words were clear enough to make her pause. He tilted his head slightly, studying her as though she were a puzzle he couldn't quite solve. "And too loud."

Aria blinked, momentarily caught off guard. "Well, excuse me for panicking. I've been dragged into some kind of fever dream, tied up, and paraded through your village like some trophy."

He raised an eyebrow but said nothing, his silence infuriatingly calm.

"Who are you, anyway?" she demanded, leaning forward. "Another guard? Or are you here to tell me more cryptic nonsense about Seluna and shattered queens?"

"My name is Torin," he said evenly. His gaze didn't waver. "I'm here to watch you."

"Watch me?" Aria scoffed. "What, am I a flight risk with my hands tied? Or are you expecting me to sprout wings and fly out of here?"

Torin's expression flickered—just for a moment—as though he were suppressing a smirk. "You might try. I wouldn't put it past you."

Her sarcasm faltered, and she frowned. "Look," she began, her tone softening. "I don't know what you think I am, but I don't belong here. Whatever you saw—whatever you think—you've made a mistake."

Torin leaned back slightly, his arms still crossed. "A mistake? You appeared at the temple. You triggered the relic. You came here." His voice was calm, but there was an edge to it, like a blade hidden beneath a layer of cloth. "The Shattered Queen's prophecy speaks of your arrival."

"I don't even know what that means!" Aria shot back, her frustration boiling over. "I didn't ask for this. I didn't choose to be here."

"And yet, here you are," Torin replied, his voice steady. "The people believe you. They see the signs."

She stared at him, her mouth opening and closing as she struggled to find the right words. "The people believe…?" she echoed, incredulous. "Do you? Do you actually think I'm this—this queen?"

Torin's silence was deafening. He studied her for a long moment, his eyes narrowing slightly as though searching for a hidden truth. Finally, he said, "What I believe doesn't matter. What the prophecy says does."

Aria slumped back against the bench, letting out a bitter laugh. "Great. So I'm just a pawn in some ancient prophecy? That's comforting."

Torin stepped closer, his gaze hardening. "You're not a pawn. You're a symbol. Whether you like it or not, these people will follow you—or fear you."

"Fear me?" she repeated, her voice cracking. "I don't want anyone to fear me. I just want to go home."

"Home." The word seemed to linger in the air. Torin's expression softened slightly, though his tone remained firm. "If what the elders say is true, you can't go back. Not yet."

Aria's throat tightened, and she looked away, blinking rapidly. "This is insane," she muttered, her voice barely above a whisper. "I don't know how to fix your prophecy. I'm not even sure I believe in it."

"Then learn," Torin said, his tone blunt but not unkind. "Because if you fail, it won't just be your life that ends."

His words hung heavy in the air, and for the first time, Aria felt the full weight of the situation pressing down on her. She looked back at Torin, meeting his gaze. Despite his stern demeanor, there was something in his eyes—something almost human.

"Help me," she said quietly. "If you think I'm this... symbol, then help me figure out what I'm supposed to do."

Torin's jaw tightened, and he nodded once. "I'll do my duty," he said. "But don't expect me to believe in miracles."

"Good," Aria replied, a faint smirk tugging at her lips despite the fear coiling in her chest. "Because I don't either."

For the first time, a ghost of a smile flickered across Torin's face before it disappeared, replaced by his stoic mask. "Get some rest," he said, turning toward the door. "Tomorrow, we begin."

And with that, he was gone, leaving Aria alone with her thoughts and the ominous promise of what lay ahead.

The village square was alive with murmurs as the crowd gathered under the dim glow of firelight. Aria stood in the center, her wrists still bound, flanked by two warriors who had dragged her here from the holding hut. She was exhausted, her legs trembling under the weight of her fear and confusion. Around her, the villagers whispered in their strange language, their eyes flicking toward her with a mixture of awe and unease.

At the far end of the square, a semi-circle of elders sat atop carved wooden chairs that were raised slightly above the gathering. Their faces were weathered, their expressions inscrutable. Each elder wore a mantle of woven vines and beads, and their gazes bore into Aria with an intensity that made her skin crawl.

"I don't know why I'm here," Aria said, her voice shaking as she addressed the elders. "This has to be some kind of mistake."

Her words elicited a ripple of murmurs from the crowd. One of the elders, a woman with silver hair twisted into an elaborate braid, raised her hand, and the voices quieted instantly. She spoke in a measured, melodic tone, her eyes never leaving Aria. Though Aria couldn't understand the words, the authority in the woman's voice was unmistakable.

Aria turned to Torin, who stood nearby, his arms crossed and his expression as impassive as ever. "Can you please tell them I'm not who they think I am? I'm just... I'm nobody. A historian. I don't belong here."

Torin's gaze didn't waver. "They don't see it that way."

"Well, maybe they should," Aria snapped, her frustration boiling over. She turned back to the elders. "Listen, I don't know what this prophecy is, but I'm not your Shattered Queen. I don't even know what that means!"

Another elder, a wiry man with deep-set eyes and a voice like gravel, spoke next. His words were clipped, deliberate, and filled with an undercurrent of suspicion. He gestured toward Aria, his weathered hand trembling slightly, as though the weight of his words carried an unbearable burden.

Torin stepped forward, translating calmly. "He says you appeared at the Temple of Seluna, where no outsider has tread in generations. You activated the relic—something only one of destiny could do."

"I didn't activate anything!" Aria exclaimed. "I touched something I shouldn't have, and now I'm stuck here!"

The elder's voice grew sharper, and Torin translated again. "He says the prophecy foretold of a queen who would return to Ilyria in its darkest hour. A queen who could unite the fractured tribes or doom them all."

"That's ridiculous!" Aria shouted, her desperation mounting. "I'm not a queen! I'm not a savior or a destroyer or whatever you think I am. I'm just—"

"Enough," Torin interrupted quietly but firmly. His gaze shifted to the silver-haired elder, who had remained silent during the exchange. "They're waiting for her decree."

The elder woman stood, her movements slow but deliberate. She stepped down from her platform, approaching Aria with a grace that belied her age. The crowd hushed as she moved, their collective breath held in anticipation.

Aria stiffened as the woman stopped in front of her, their eyes locking. The elder's gaze was piercing, as though she could see straight through Aria's protests, her fears, her very soul. Without speaking, the elder reached out, her gnarled fingers brushing Aria's forehead lightly. The touch sent a shiver down Aria's spine.

The elder finally spoke, her voice carrying a reverent weight. She uttered a string of words, and Torin translated softly beside her.

"She says you are the Shattered Queen reborn," Torin murmured. "A figure of great power. And great danger."

Aria's heart sank. "No. She's wrong. She has to be."

The elder woman continued, her tone unyielding. Torin's voice was quieter now, almost reluctant. "She says your arrival marks the turning point. You will either bring salvation… or ruin."

The murmurs in the crowd grew louder, a mixture of fear and hope. Aria's knees buckled slightly, and she shook her head, her voice barely above a whisper. "This can't be happening. I can't be her."

The elder stepped back, her decree final. She turned and spoke to the crowd, her words ringing out over their whispers. Torin didn't translate this time, but Aria didn't need him to. The meaning was clear. Whatever she said, the people believed her.

The villagers dropped to their knees, bowing their heads in unison. It was a display of reverence that felt suffocating, a weight Aria wasn't prepared to carry. She looked around, her eyes wide, panic rising in her chest.

"This is a mistake!" she shouted, her voice cracking. "I can't help you! I don't know how!"

Torin stepped closer, his presence steady amidst the chaos. "They won't listen to that," he said quietly. "They've already decided."

Aria turned to him, her eyes blazing. "You don't believe this, do you?"

He hesitated, the first crack in his stoic demeanor. "What I believe doesn't matter," he said finally. "This is your fate now."

The elder woman spoke one last time, her voice rising in a solemn chant. The villagers echoed her words, their collective voice sending a shiver down Aria's spine. Whatever the chant meant, it sounded final.

Aria's shoulders sagged as the weight of their expectations settled over her. Fate or not, she was trapped. The Shattered Queen they sought was a myth—but now, she was their reality.

The crackling of the ceremonial fire filled the silence as Aria stood on the wide, circular platform in the center of the Verdant Clans' village. The villagers formed a ring around her, their faces lit with a mixture of expectation and fear. The elders stood closest to the fire, their expressions unreadable, their gazes fixed on her. The weight of their collective stares pressed against Aria like an invisible force.

"I don't want to do this," Aria said, her voice trembling as she turned to Torin, who stood just behind her. "I don't even know what this is."

Torin's face was as unreadable as ever. "It's a test," he said. "To prove if you are who they believe you to be."

"I've already told you, I'm not," she hissed, her voice low.

His gaze flicked toward the elders. "That's not for me to decide. Or them."

Her stomach churned. "What happens if I fail?" she whispered.

Torin's jaw tightened slightly. "Don't fail."

Before she could protest, one of the elders, the silver-haired woman from earlier, raised her hands and spoke in a commanding tone. Her voice was melodic, almost hypnotic, as it wove through the night air. The villagers murmured in response, their voices rising and falling in unison.

"Torin," Aria said urgently, stepping closer to him. "What is she saying?"

"She's calling on the essence," he replied. "The magic of this place. If you are truly connected to the prophecy, the essence will respond."

"And if it doesn't?"

Torin met her eyes, his expression softening ever so slightly. "It will."

A younger elder approached, holding a shallow bowl carved from stone. The contents shimmered faintly, a liquid that seemed to pulse with an inner glow. He handed the bowl to the silver-haired elder, who approached Aria slowly, her movements deliberate.

"What is that?" Aria asked, her voice rising with panic.

"Essence water," Torin explained. "Drawn from the sacred pools deep in the jungle."

The elder dipped her fingers into the liquid, then gestured for Aria to kneel. Aria hesitated, glancing at Torin.

"Do it," he said quietly. "It's the only way."

She sank to her knees, her heart pounding as the elder stepped closer. The woman spoke softly, the words foreign but soothing. She dipped her fingers into the bowl again and pressed them against Aria's forehead, leaving cool trails of the glowing liquid on her skin.

"This is insane," Aria muttered under her breath.

"Quiet," Torin said sharply.

The elder began to chant, her voice low and rhythmic, the sound reverberating through the space. The villagers joined in, their voices blending into a haunting melody that sent a shiver down Aria's spine. The fire in the center of the platform flared brighter, its orange glow shifting to a deep, unnatural green.

Aria's breath hitched. "What's happening?"

Torin crouched beside her, his voice low. "It's starting. Don't fight it."

"Fight what?" she demanded, but before he could answer, a strange warmth spread from her forehead, where the essence water had been applied. It traveled down her spine, tingling as it moved through her body. She gasped, her hands gripping the edge of the platform for support.

"Something's wrong," she said, her voice tight. "This doesn't feel right."

"It's the essence," Torin said. "Let it in."

The warmth intensified, growing into a pulsing heat that seemed to radiate outward. Her vision blurred, the chanting fading into the background as an overwhelming surge of energy coursed through her. Images flashed before her eyes—vivid, otherworldly scenes she couldn't comprehend. A figure cloaked in light, standing atop a battlefield. Fractured landscapes, divided by chasms of glowing energy. And a crown, jagged and gleaming, shattering into pieces before reforming.

Aria cried out, clutching her head as the visions overwhelmed her. "Stop! Make it stop!"

The silver-haired elder's chant grew louder, her voice cutting through the haze. The villagers' chorus reached a crescendo, and the fire flared again, brighter and higher than before. Aria's body jerked as the energy reached its peak, a blinding light erupting from her chest and casting the entire square in an ethereal glow.

Then, as suddenly as it began, it was over. The fire returned to its normal hue, and the glow around Aria faded. She collapsed forward, catching herself with trembling arms. Her breaths came in ragged gasps, her body drenched in sweat.

The crowd was silent, the air thick with awe. Slowly, the villagers fell to their knees, bowing their heads as one. The elders exchanged solemn looks before the silver-haired woman stepped forward, speaking in a tone of quiet reverence.

Torin knelt beside Aria, his hand resting lightly on her shoulder. "She says the essence has accepted you."

Aria shook her head weakly. "No… no. That wasn't acceptance. That was…" She couldn't find the words, her mind reeling from the experience.

"You saw something," Torin said, his voice soft but insistent. "What was it?"

"I don't know," she whispered. "It was… fragments. A crown, light, and—and destruction."

Torin's eyes darkened, but he said nothing. The silver-haired elder continued speaking, her voice rising with conviction.

"She says you are the Shattered Queen reborn," Torin translated. "The prophecy is clear now. They believe you will bring balance. Or ruin."

Aria stared at him, her breath catching. "I can't do this."

"You don't have a choice," Torin said, his tone firm but not unkind. "Neither do they."

The villagers rose, their faces alight with a mix of hope and fear. The silver-haired elder bowed deeply to Aria, murmuring words that needed no translation.

Fate, it seemed, had already decided.

The village was quiet now, save for the faint crackle of the fire in the square and the soft hum of nocturnal creatures in the jungle beyond. Aria sat on the same low bench in the hut where she'd been held earlier, her knees drawn to her chest and her wrists free but sore from the ropes that had bound them. Her whole body trembled, not from cold but from the memory of the ceremony—the fire, the chanting, the surge of power that had coursed through her veins like liquid light.

It had felt so real. Too real.

The door creaked open, and she looked up to see Torin step inside. His imposing frame was a shadow against the firelight outside, his expression unreadable as always. He shut the door behind him and leaned against it, arms crossed.

"I'm not her," Aria said abruptly, her voice hoarse. "Whatever they think I am, they're wrong."

Torin raised an eyebrow, but his face remained calm. "You felt the essence."

"That doesn't mean anything," she shot back. "Maybe it's just… some kind of hallucination, or a reaction to whatever they put on my forehead."

His lips quirked into a humorless smile. "A hallucination doesn't make the fire glow or bring an entire village to its knees."

Her chest tightened. "No, but—" She faltered, shaking her head. "This isn't real. It can't be. I touched a relic in a temple, and now I'm here, surrounded by people who think I'm some kind of savior. That doesn't happen. It's not possible."

Torin pushed off the door and stepped closer, his boots thudding softly against the wooden floor. "And yet, here you are."

"That's not an answer!" she snapped, her voice rising. "You don't get to just say, 'It's fate,' and expect me to accept it. I need to go home. There has to be a way."

Torin sighed, a faint trace of impatience flickering across his face. "And if there isn't?"

Her heart skipped a beat. "There has to be," she said again, but the conviction in her voice wavered. "You don't understand. My world—it's not like this. I don't belong here. I belong back there."

Torin sat down on a stool across from her, resting his forearms on his knees. "What do you think is waiting for you back there?" he asked, his tone measured.

"Everything!" she exclaimed. "My life, my work… my world."

"And yet, you touched the relic," Torin said. "Why?"

She opened her mouth to respond but hesitated. The truth sat heavy in her chest. "I… I didn't know what would happen."

His gaze sharpened. "You didn't think it might bring you here?"

"No!" she said, shaking her head vehemently. "I thought it was just an artifact. A piece of history to study, not some magical doorway."

Torin leaned back, his expression softening into something almost pitying. "If it wasn't fate, then why did you go to the temple at all?"

"Because it's my job!" she snapped. "I'm a historian. I study ruins, relics, myths. That's all this was supposed to be—just another myth."

"And now it isn't." His words landed like a blow, cutting through her protests.

She stared at him, her breath quick and shallow. "I didn't ask for this," she whispered. "I didn't ask to be dragged into some prophecy I don't believe in."

"Fate doesn't ask," Torin said simply. "It moves, whether you believe in it or not."

Aria rubbed her hands over her face, her frustration mounting. "How can you be so calm about this? You're just going to stand there and tell me this is all part of some plan?"

"I'm calm because I've seen this before," Torin said. His tone was steady, almost weary. "The prophecy is older than any of us. The elders have spoken of it my entire life. And now you're here, just as they said you would be."

She let out a hollow laugh. "And you believe them? Just like that?"

"I believe what I see," he replied. "And what I saw tonight… was not nothing."

His words sent a chill down her spine. She looked away, her hands curling into fists. "I just want to go home," she said, her voice trembling. "Can't you understand that?"

For a moment, Torin was silent. Then he said, softly, "Home is a place you make, not a place you go back to."

She whipped her head around to glare at him. "That's easy for you to say. This is your home."

"It was my home long before you arrived," he admitted. "And it will be here long after you leave, if that's your choice. But until then, you have a role to play."

She scoffed, tears burning at the corners of her eyes. "I didn't ask for a role."

"No one does," Torin said, his voice firm but not unkind. He stood, his shadow falling over her as he moved toward the door. "Get some rest. Tomorrow, you'll begin to understand."

He opened the door, pausing briefly before stepping outside. "And for what it's worth," he said, glancing over his shoulder, "the people here don't see you as a burden. They see you as hope. That's more than most people get."

With that, he left, leaving Aria alone with her thoughts. The fire outside cast flickering shadows across the room, but the light felt far away, distant, like the world she knew. For the first time, she realized that "home" might be slipping further out of reach with every passing moment.

Chapter 3
Among Strangers

The jungle's oppressive heat pressed down on Aria as she trudged along the narrow path, her legs aching from days of endless walking. Sweat trickled down her back, soaking into her already damp clothes. She swatted at a mosquito buzzing near her ear and groaned in frustration.

"This is barbaric," she muttered under her breath, sidestepping a particularly large root that snaked across the trail. "No tents, no beds, no showers… How do any of you survive out here?"

Torin, walking a few paces ahead, didn't look back. "We survive because we don't complain," he said, his tone as dry as the leather armor he wore.

Aria scowled at his broad back. "Easy for you to say. You grew up in this. I grew up in a world with air conditioning and takeout."

Torin stopped abruptly and turned to face her, his expression impassive. "You keep saying things like that—air conditioning, takeout—but they mean nothing to me. Focus on the here and now."

"The 'here and now' sucks," Aria shot back, folding her arms.

Torin's eyes narrowed. "You can whine all you want, but it won't make the jungle easier to survive."

"Maybe if you actually explained what we're doing, I wouldn't have to 'whine,'" she snapped. "We've been walking for three days with no clear destination. What are we even looking for?"

Torin stepped closer, his voice low and firm. "We're looking for answers. The ruins ahead might hold another fragment of the prophecy. Or would you prefer to sit in the village and wait for someone else to find them?"

Aria hesitated, his words hitting a nerve. She looked away, muttering, "I didn't ask to be dragged into this."

"You've said that already." Torin turned and began walking again. "It doesn't change anything."

Frustration simmered in her chest, but she bit back another retort and followed. The jungle seemed to close in around them as the hours dragged on. The dense foliage muffled the sound of their footsteps, leaving only the occasional rustle of leaves or the distant call of a bird to break the silence.

Then came a sound that didn't belong—a low, guttural growl that froze Aria mid-step.

"Did you hear that?" she whispered, her voice barely audible.

Torin raised a hand, signaling for her to stay quiet. His other hand went to the hilt of his blade as he scanned the underbrush. The growl came again, closer this time, followed by the distinct crunch of branches underfoot.

"What is it?" Aria hissed, her heart pounding.

Torin didn't answer. Instead, he drew his weapon, the steel gleaming faintly in the dappled sunlight. "Stay behind me," he ordered.

Before she could respond, a massive creature burst through the undergrowth, its eyes gleaming with feral hunger. It was unlike anything Aria had ever seen—resembling a panther, but larger, its black fur rippling with a faint, otherworldly glow. Its claws raked the ground as it stalked toward them, its growl vibrating through the air.

"Stay back!" Torin barked, placing himself between Aria and the beast.

The creature lunged, and Torin dodged, slashing at its flank. His blade connected, but the beast barely flinched, its growl deepening into a snarl. It swiped at him with claws like daggers, and Torin narrowly avoided the blow, his movements quick but strained.

Aria stumbled backward, her breathing rapid. "What do I do?" she shouted, panic lacing her voice.

"Run!" Torin shouted, dodging another swipe. "Get out of here!"

But Aria didn't run. Something deep within her—instinct or madness, she wasn't sure—compelled her to stay. Her hands trembled as she remembered the ceremony, the surge of energy that had coursed through her. She reached out, her mind racing.

"Come on," she whispered to herself, her voice shaky. "If you're going to do something, do it now."

The beast turned its glowing eyes on her, its body coiling as it prepared to pounce. Aria raised her hands, her heart hammering against her ribs. She felt a faint warmth in her palms, growing stronger with each breath.

The creature leapt, but before it could reach her, vines erupted from the ground, twisting around its limbs and pulling it to the forest floor. The beast thrashed and snarled, but the vines held firm, their grip tightening as though responding to her will.

Torin turned, his eyes widening at the sight. "Aria," he said, his voice filled with equal parts shock and caution. "What are you doing?"

"I don't know!" she shouted, her focus split between the writhing creature and the strange energy pulsing through her. "But it's working!"

The beast let out a final, guttural snarl before slumping to the ground, the fight draining from its body. The vines loosened and retreated into the soil, leaving the jungle eerily silent.

Aria collapsed to her knees, her chest heaving. Torin approached slowly, his blade still in hand but lowered. "Are you hurt?" he asked, his voice quieter now.

She shook her head, unable to speak. Her hands still tingled with residual energy, and her mind reeled from what had just happened.

Torin knelt beside her, his expression unreadable. "You saved us," he said after a moment. "That power… it wasn't luck."

"I don't want this," she whispered, her voice barely audible. "I don't want any of this."

Torin's gaze softened, and he placed a hand on her shoulder. "It doesn't matter what you want. It's yours now. Learn to use it—or it will destroy you."

His words hung heavy in the air as Aria stared at the ground, the reality of her situation sinking deeper with every passing second. She had saved them, but at what cost? The world she had once known felt further away than ever.

The jungle exhaled around them, the quiet punctuated only by the distant chirp of insects and the rustle of leaves. Aria trudged a few steps behind Torin, her legs aching and her mind replaying the attack in an endless loop. Every muscle in her body felt like it had been pulled taut and then released, leaving her exhausted but alive. The vines—*her* vines—had saved them both.

Torin walked ahead in silence, his blade now sheathed but his posture still tense. He paused at a wide, moss-covered tree, his sharp gaze scanning the shadows before gesturing for Aria to catch up.

"You're falling behind," he said, his voice neutral but lacking the usual edge of irritation.

Aria swallowed her exhaustion and quickened her pace. "I just fought off a glowing panther with magic I didn't know I had. Forgive me if I'm not sprinting."

Torin didn't respond immediately. Instead, he adjusted the strap of his pack and gestured toward the path. "We'll set up camp ahead. It's safer there."

She snorted, brushing a stray leaf from her hair. "Define 'safer.' Because if another one of those things shows up, I might not have a miracle left."

Torin turned to her, his dark eyes narrowing slightly. "What you did back there wasn't a miracle. It was control."

"Control?" she repeated, incredulous. "That didn't feel like control. It felt like panic mixed with dumb luck."

He considered her words for a moment, then nodded. "Control born of instinct, then. But luck only gets you so far."

Aria frowned, watching as he moved ahead. His tone wasn't scolding, and that was a shift. She filed it away as they pressed forward. The path narrowed, the thick canopy above creating a tunnel of green light. Torin slowed, his steps deliberate, and motioned for her to stop.

"Watch this," he said, crouching low. His hand hovered over a patch of what looked like innocuous moss. "This plant is called Widow's Whisper. Looks harmless, but its spores are deadly. Step too close, and it'll release them."

Aria stiffened, instinctively stepping back. "Deadly how?"

"They paralyze you first," Torin explained. "Then they slowly shut down your lungs."

She grimaced, giving the moss an even wider berth. "Lovely. What's the lesson here? Don't step on anything green?"

"The lesson," Torin said, standing and dusting his hands, "is to be aware. This jungle doesn't forgive carelessness. It's alive, and it will test you."

Aria hesitated, then nodded. "Thanks for the warning. Though I'm starting to think you enjoy scaring me."

His lips twitched—just barely—and he turned without a word, continuing down the trail. For a moment, she thought she might have imagined the almost-smile.

They reached a clearing not long after, the dense vegetation giving way to a small, sun-dappled space where Torin gestured for her to sit. He unslung his pack and pulled out a waterskin, tossing it to her.

"Drink," he said. "You'll need it."

Aria caught it clumsily and took a long sip. The water was cool and refreshing, though it did little to quell her nerves. She handed the skin back. "So, this is the part where you tell me I should've run instead of trying to be a hero, right?"

Torin sat on a nearby rock, his expression thoughtful. "If you'd run, we'd both be dead."

The bluntness of his words startled her. She blinked, unsure how to respond. "That's… not what I expected you to say."

"I don't waste time on false gratitude," he said. "But you acted. That's more than most would've done."

The faintest warmth of pride stirred in her chest, though she quickly squashed it. "Well, don't get used to it. I didn't exactly have a choice."

"No one does," Torin replied simply. "But you used what you had. That's more important than bravery."

Aria studied him, her head tilting slightly. "You almost sound like you're complimenting me."

"Don't let it go to your head," he said, though there was no bite to his tone. He stood, scanning the clearing. "Now, pay attention. This spot is safe for the night, but not if you leave food out or light a fire too large."

"More jungle wisdom?" she asked, unable to keep the sarcasm from her voice.

"Wisdom keeps you alive," Torin replied, his tone firm. "I'll teach you what I can, but survival is your responsibility."

She nodded, realizing this was the closest thing to a truce they'd had since meeting. "Alright," she said quietly. "Teach me."

He glanced at her, his expression unreadable, but after a moment, he gave a curt nod. "We'll start with setting up camp. Then I'll show you how to use the jungle's sounds to tell what's coming."

As he began explaining the basics of their makeshift shelter, Aria felt a small shift between them. Torin's sharp edges weren't gone, but they had softened, just enough to let her see the man behind the stoicism. And for the first time, she wondered if surviving this place might not be impossible after all.

The jungle path stretched before them, narrow and winding, flanked by dense vegetation that seemed to hum with life. The heat of the day had waned, leaving the air heavy but cooler, the sun dipping below the horizon. Aria followed closely behind Torin, her feet dragging slightly on the uneven terrain. Her body still ached from days of travel, and her mind was clouded with thoughts of what lay ahead.

For a while, neither of them spoke. The silence between them was no longer as sharp-edged as it had been, but it still carried an unspoken tension. Aria glanced at Torin's back, his movements sure and practiced, each step purposeful. She cleared her throat softly, breaking the quiet.

"So," she began, her voice tentative, "this prophecy... the Shattered Queen... What exactly is it? I think I deserve to know."

Torin slowed his pace but didn't stop. "You know more than you think," he said, his tone even. "You've seen the signs. You've felt the essence."

"That doesn't explain anything," Aria countered, frustration creeping into her voice. "You can't just say 'fate' and expect me to accept it like everyone else."

Torin sighed and came to a halt, turning to face her. His expression was guarded, but there was no disdain in his gaze—only a quiet resolve. "The Shattered Queen was more than a ruler. She was a force that united Ilyria during its darkest time. But she was also the reason it fractured."

Aria frowned, crossing her arms. "That's… contradictory."

"She was human," Torin replied simply. "Humans are contradictory." He gestured for her to follow and resumed walking. "The Queen wielded immense power—power tied to the essence of this world. She used it to bring peace, but it came at a cost."

"What kind of cost?" Aria pressed, stepping over a root that jutted across the path.

"Her life," Torin said. "To seal the rifts that were tearing this world apart, she sacrificed herself. But the rifts didn't stay sealed. Without her, the tribes fell into chaos. Divisions formed, alliances crumbled. The Verdant Clans believe her spirit will return when the rifts threaten Ilyria again."

"And they think that's me?" Aria asked, her voice softening. "Because I touched some relic and survived?"

"It's not just the relic," Torin said. "The elders see the signs. The essence responded to you during the ceremony. These aren't coincidences."

She walked in silence for a moment, letting his words sink in. "What if they're wrong?" she asked finally. "What if I'm just… a random person who doesn't belong here?"

Torin glanced at her, his expression unreadable. "What if they're not?"

Aria stopped, shaking her head. "You don't understand. I'm not a leader. I've never led anyone, let alone saved a world."

Torin turned to face her, his voice calm but firm. "Do you think the Shattered Queen wanted to lead? To save anyone? History doesn't record what she wanted, only what she did."

"That's a convenient way to avoid asking questions," Aria muttered.

"It's the truth," he said simply. "And now it's your truth."

She let out a bitter laugh, her arms dropping to her sides. "I didn't ask for this."

"No one ever does," Torin replied, his voice softer now. "But you're here. And that means something to these people."

Aria exhaled heavily, running a hand through her tangled hair. "It doesn't feel real. Any of it. Back home, I was just… normal. A nobody."

"You weren't a nobody," Torin said, his tone shifting slightly. "Not if fate brought you here."

She looked at him, her brow furrowed. "Do you really believe in fate? Or are you just saying that because it's what your people believe?"

Torin paused, his gaze dropping briefly to the ground. "I believe in what I see," he said finally. "And what I've seen is enough."

"Enough for you, maybe," Aria said. "But I didn't grow up with stories of prophecies and essence magic. I grew up in a world where nothing like this exists."

Torin studied her for a moment, then nodded. "That's why you're scared."

Her jaw tightened, but she didn't deny it. "Wouldn't you be?"

"I was," he admitted quietly. "When I first became a warrior. When I took up my blade and swore to protect my people, I didn't know if I could. But I did it because someone had to."

"That's not the same," Aria said. "You trained for this. I'm just… me."

"And yet you saved us from the beast," Torin said. "You acted when you could have run. That's more than most would do."

She looked away, the weight of his words pressing down on her. "I don't know if I can do this," she said softly.

Torin stepped closer, his voice steady but not unkind. "You don't have to know yet. You just have to try."

For a long moment, they stood in silence, the jungle around them humming with life. Aria finally nodded, though her uncertainty lingered in her eyes.

"Alright," she said quietly. "I'll try."

Torin turned and started walking again, his pace unhurried. "Good," he said. "Because the next part of this journey isn't going to get any easier."

Aria followed, the weight of the Shattered Queen's legacy settling heavily on her shoulders. It wasn't a role she wanted, but perhaps, she thought, it was one she could learn to carry.

The campfire crackled softly, its warm light casting flickering shadows against the surrounding trees. The jungle night was alive with distant sounds—chirping insects, the rustle of unseen creatures moving through the undergrowth, and the faint whisper of a breeze that barely stirred the humid air. Aria sat cross-legged on the ground, her arms wrapped around her knees, the firelight highlighting the tension in her shoulders.

Across from her, Torin tended to the fire, methodically adding small branches to the flames.

She broke the silence first. "Do you ever stop looking like the world's about to end?"

Torin glanced up, his expression as impassive as ever. "The world is always ending somewhere."

Aria snorted, resting her chin on her knees. "That's… comforting."

"You wanted honesty," Torin said, his tone clipped. He poked the fire with a stick, sending sparks spiraling into the night. "You should've expected it wouldn't be comforting."

Aria rolled her eyes but didn't reply immediately. She watched the fire instead, her mind swirling with unspoken questions. The weight of the day's revelations sat heavily on her, but Torin's presence, though sharp-edged, was beginning to feel less oppressive. She took a deep breath and spoke again, her voice softer this time.

"Do you believe it?" she asked. "The prophecy, I mean. That I'm the Shattered Queen reborn."

Torin stilled, the stick in his hand poised above the flames. He didn't answer right away, his gaze fixed on the fire. "Belief isn't as simple as yes or no," he said finally.

"That's a convenient dodge," Aria said, leaning back on her hands. "Try again."

He smirked faintly—just enough for her to notice. "I believe the elders are wise," he said. "I believe in the essence and the power it holds. But the prophecy… it's a story. A hope. Stories can be dangerous."

Aria tilted her head, surprised by the admission. "Dangerous how?"

"Because people cling to them," he said, his voice quieter now. "They make decisions based on faith, not reality. They see what they want to see and ignore what doesn't fit."

She studied him, sensing a deeper conflict behind his words. "So, you don't think I'm her."

Torin met her gaze then, his dark eyes steady. "I think you're here. I think the essence responded to you. Whether that makes you the Shattered Queen or something else… I don't know."

The honesty in his voice caught her off guard. She shifted her weight, the hard ground beneath her suddenly uncomfortable. "You don't sound like someone who blindly follows the elders," she said carefully.

"I don't," he replied. "But I respect them. Their guidance has kept the clans alive for generations."

"And now their guidance is telling everyone to pin their hopes on me," Aria said bitterly. "A complete stranger who didn't even know this place existed a week ago."

Torin nodded, his expression softening. "It's not fair," he admitted. "But fairness doesn't matter. What matters is what you do with it."

She laughed, though the sound was hollow. "Great. No pressure."

For a moment, silence stretched between them, broken only by the fire's crackling. Torin leaned back, resting his forearms on his knees. His voice, when he spoke again, was quieter, almost reflective.

"When I was a boy," he said, "my father used to tell me the story of the Shattered Queen. How she united the tribes, how she fought to save this world. He believed she'd come back someday."

Aria looked at him, surprised by the personal note in his words. "What about you? Did you believe him?"

Torin hesitated, then shook his head. "No. I thought it was just a story. A way to give people hope when things were hard."

"And now?"

"Now…" He sighed, rubbing a hand over his jaw. "Now I'm not sure. I've seen things I can't explain. Things that make me wonder if my father was right."

Aria's chest tightened at the vulnerability in his tone. She didn't know what to say, so she settled for the truth. "For what it's worth," she said quietly, "I don't want to be her. Or anyone, really. I just want to go home."

Torin's gaze softened, and for the first time, his stoic mask seemed to crack. "I know," he said. "But wanting doesn't change what is."

Her eyes stung, but she blinked quickly, forcing the tears away. "It doesn't feel real," she admitted. "Any of it. This place, the prophecy… me. It feels like I'm stuck in someone else's story."

"Maybe you are," Torin said. "But you're here now. And whether you like it or not, you have a role to play."

She swallowed hard, the firelight dancing in her vision. "And you? What's your role?"

"To keep you alive long enough to figure out yours," he said, his tone tinged with dry humor.

A reluctant smile tugged at her lips. "Sounds thrilling."

Torin's lips curved into a faint smirk. "You'll get used to it."

She wasn't sure she believed him, but for the first time, she felt a sliver of something she hadn't expected: trust. It was fragile, tentative, but it was there. And in the midst of the uncertainty that surrounded her, it was enough. For now.

Chapter 4
The Mark of Seluna

The low hum of voices outside the hut carried through the woven walls, blending with the crackle of torches and the distant rhythm of drums. Aria sat cross-legged on a soft mat of dried leaves, her wrists loosely bound with a silken cord. The restraints weren't tight enough to hurt, but their presence was unnerving nonetheless. She flexed her fingers, feeling the material bite gently into her skin.

"Do they always do this?" she asked, her voice wavering. "The whole tying-people-up thing? Is it symbolic or just overkill?"

Torin stood near the doorway, his broad frame silhouetted against the warm torchlight streaming through the entrance. He didn't answer right away, his gaze fixed on the movements of the elders bustling around her. They spoke in their flowing, melodic tongue, their voices calm yet purposeful as they arranged bowls of glowing liquid and strange artifacts around the room.

"Torin?" Aria pressed, her tone sharper now.

"Yes," he said finally, glancing at her. His voice was flat, practical. "It's symbolic. And necessary."

"Necessary for what, exactly?" She twisted her hands, lifting the cord slightly. "For this? Is this supposed to make me feel… what, humble? Like a sacrificial lamb?"

Torin sighed and stepped closer, crouching beside her. His dark eyes scanned her face, unreadable as ever. "It's not for you. It's for them. The binding is a gesture—proof that you surrender to the will of the prophecy. They need to believe in this."

"And what if I don't believe in it?" Aria shot back, her voice low but fierce. "I don't even know what this prophecy is supposed to be."

Torin's jaw tightened. He leaned in slightly, his voice dropping to a whisper. "Whether you believe it or not doesn't matter. To them, you're Seluna's chosen. Tonight will prove if you are who they think you are."

Aria frowned, her stomach twisting. "And if I'm not?"

He didn't answer, but the flicker in his eyes was enough. She bit her lip, glancing toward the elders. One of them, an older woman with silver streaks in her braids and an elaborate headdress of feathers and beads, stepped forward and knelt in front of Aria. Her weathered hands held a small bowl filled with a faintly glowing blue liquid.

The elder spoke softly, her words flowing like water. She gestured to the bowl, then to Aria, her expression expectant.

"What's she saying?" Aria whispered, shifting uncomfortably.

Torin straightened. "She's asking you to drink. It's part of the ritual."

"Of course it is," Aria muttered under her breath. She eyed the liquid warily, its faint luminescence casting rippling patterns on the walls. "What's in it?"

"Essence," Torin replied. "A purified form, mixed with herbs. It's meant to connect you to the prophecy."

"Connect me," she repeated, her tone dry. "That sounds ominous."

Torin's patience was thinning. "Just drink it. Refusing will only make things worse."

Aria hesitated, her gaze darting between Torin and the elder. "What happens if it kills me?"

"It won't," Torin said firmly. "The elders wouldn't risk the wrath of Seluna."

"That's... not as comforting as you think it is."

The elder shifted slightly, holding the bowl closer. Her eyes locked with Aria's, and for a moment, the room seemed to grow quieter, the hum of voices outside fading into the background. Aria swallowed hard. There was no malice in the woman's expression, only an unwavering belief that made Aria's chest tighten. These people truly thought she was something more than herself. Something divine.

With a resigned sigh, Aria reached out, her bound hands making the movement awkward. She took the bowl and brought it to her lips. The liquid was cool and tasted faintly of earth and flowers, the glowing warmth spreading through her throat and chest as she swallowed.

The elder murmured a word Aria didn't understand, bowing her head in approval before retreating. The others moved in, their hands working quickly to adorn her with intricate designs painted onto her skin. The brushes tickled slightly, and Aria tried not to flinch.

"Torin," she said, her voice softer now. "What if… what if they're wrong? What if this doesn't prove anything?"

Torin's gaze flicked toward the elders before returning to her. "It will prove what they need it to prove."

"That's not an answer," she snapped.

"It's the only one you're getting," he replied, his tone firm but not unkind. "Just do as they ask. Let the ritual play out."

"And if I screw it up?"

"You won't," he said simply, though his eyes betrayed a sliver of doubt.

Aria let out a bitter laugh. "Glad you have so much faith in me."

"It's not faith in you," Torin said, standing and returning to his post by the doorway. "It's faith in the prophecy."

Aria fell silent, her fingers clenching and unclenching against the cord around her wrists. The hum of the elders' chants grew louder, filling the small hut with an almost tangible energy. The symbols they painted onto her skin seemed to glow faintly in the firelight, and she felt the weight of their belief settle heavily on her shoulders.

For the first time, she realized this wasn't just about surviving the night. It was about becoming something she wasn't sure she could be. Something they desperately needed her to be.

The night air was thick with humidity, the scent of earth and smoke mingling as torches burned brightly around the village square. Shadows flickered and danced on the woven walls of huts and the gnarled trunks of surrounding trees. The hum of the crowd, low and expectant, filled the space, rising and falling like the tide.

Aria stood at the edge of the square, her breath shallow, her wrists still bound loosely with the silken cord. Two warriors flanked her, their painted faces impassive as they motioned her forward. Her feet felt like lead, her steps hesitant as she was guided into the circle of torchlight.

The villagers, clad in feathers and beads, parted as she approached, their eyes wide with awe—or was it fear? She couldn't tell. Murmurs rippled through the crowd, a single word repeated over and over: "Seluna."

Her heart thudded painfully in her chest. "Torin," she hissed through clenched teeth. "What's happening now? What are they saying?"

Torin appeared beside her, his expression as unreadable as ever. "They're invoking Seluna. This is the moment where you prove your connection to her."

Aria's throat went dry. "Prove? How exactly am I supposed to do that?"

He glanced at her, his voice low but firm. "By letting them believe. Don't fight it. Just follow their lead."

"That's not an answer," she whispered harshly, her eyes darting to the crowd. "What if—"

"Aria," Torin interrupted, his tone sharp enough to cut through her panic. "You're already here. Just breathe. Trust me."

Before she could respond, the eldest of the village leaders, the woman with silver-streaked braids, stepped forward, raising her arms to the sky. The crowd fell silent instantly, the weight of their collective gaze settling on Aria like a physical force.

The elder began to chant, her voice low and resonant. One by one, the other elders joined in, their tones weaving together in a haunting melody that sent a chill down Aria's spine. The villagers hummed in unison, their voices blending with the chants until the air vibrated with sound.

Torin leaned close, his voice barely audible above the rhythmic chanting. "When they motion for you to kneel, do it. Don't hesitate."

"What happens after that?" Aria asked, her voice shaking.

"You'll see."

The elder approached her, carrying a small, ornate bowl of glowing liquid. The blue essence within shimmered like liquid starlight, casting faint patterns on the ground as she moved. The crowd inhaled collectively, their murmurs rising again as the elder stopped before Aria.

"She wants you to kneel," Torin murmured.

Aria's knees felt like they might buckle on their own, but she forced herself to lower them deliberately, keeping her back straight. The elder stepped closer, dipping her fingers into the glowing essence and raising them to Aria's forehead. The cool liquid tingled against her skin, and Aria flinched at the sensation.

"Don't move," Torin warned softly.

The elder's hands moved in deliberate patterns, tracing symbols across Aria's brow, cheeks, and arms. The chanting grew louder, swelling as the villagers' voices harmonized. Aria's heart pounded as she glanced at the crowd, their faces alight with expectation.

"What are they waiting for?" she whispered, barely moving her lips.

Torin's gaze flicked to the fire in the center of the square. "The moment."

"The moment for what?" Aria demanded, but her question was swallowed by the rising chants.

The elder stepped back, raising her arms once more. The villagers' voices fell silent, leaving the air heavy with anticipation. All eyes turned to the fire, which roared higher, its flames licking toward the sky in a sudden surge of green light.

Aria's breath hitched. "Did… did I do that?"

"No," Torin said, his tone low. "But they think you did."

The crowd erupted in cheers, their voices a chaotic mix of joy and reverence. They fell to their knees, bowing toward her with their foreheads pressed to the ground. The elders began chanting again, their voices carrying the word "Seluna" like a refrain.

Aria's chest tightened. "This isn't real. This can't be real."

"It's real to them," Torin said, his voice softer now. "And that's all that matters."

She looked at him, searching his face for reassurance. "Torin, what happens if they find out I'm not—"

"They won't," he interrupted, his gaze steady. "Tonight, you are the Shattered Queen. Let them believe it. It's the only way."

The elder approached again, lifting the silken cord from Aria's wrists. She untied it with care, holding it up for the crowd to see before placing it at Aria's feet. The meaning was clear: she was no longer bound, no longer just a stranger. To these people, she was something far greater.

Aria swallowed hard, her hands trembling at her sides. The chants continued, their rhythm pulsing through her like a heartbeat. For the first time, she realized there was no escape from this. They had placed their faith in her, and whether she liked it or not, she was now part of their story.

The chanting reached a fevered pitch, the rhythms pounding in Aria's ears like a drumbeat. The green flames in the center of the square crackled wildly, casting eerie shadows that seemed to shift and twist with the pulse of the villagers' voices. The air felt thick, charged with something far more potent than the humidity she had grown used to in the jungle. It pressed against her skin, heavy and alive.

Aria tried to steady her breathing, but her chest felt tight, her heart hammering in time with the chants. She glanced toward Torin, who stood just at the edge of the circle, his expression unreadable. Their eyes met briefly, and she saw a flicker of something in his gaze—concern, maybe, or anticipation. He gave her the slightest nod, a silent command to hold steady.

The elder with the silver-streaked braids stepped forward again, her arms raised as she chanted louder than the rest. Her voice cut through the din, clear and commanding, her words incomprehensible yet undeniably powerful. She dipped her fingers back into the bowl of glowing essence, lifting it high above her head. The villagers fell silent in an instant, their collective inhalation a tangible wave of expectation.

Aria's pulse quickened as the elder approached her. The elder's weathered face was calm but intense, her eyes alight with something that looked dangerously close to worship. She murmured a string of words, then reached out, pressing her essence-coated fingers to Aria's chest, just above her heart.

The cool liquid burned like fire.

Aria gasped, her body jerking as the sensation spread through her chest, radiating outward in a wave of heat. It wasn't just physical—she could feel it in her mind, an unfamiliar presence pressing against her thoughts, whispering to her in a language she didn't know but somehow understood.

"Torin!" Her voice cracked as she staggered back, clutching at her chest. "What's happening?"

He stepped forward slightly but didn't cross into the circle. "Don't fight it, Aria. Let it happen."

"Let what happen?" she snapped, her voice rising. "I—"

Her words were cut off as a surge of images exploded behind her eyes. She stumbled, her hands flying to her head as her vision blurred. The world around her melted away, replaced by a kaleidoscope of memories that weren't her own.

A crown, gleaming gold and encrusted with jewels, shattered into a thousand pieces. A fractured world, its sky torn by jagged lines of light, burned with fire and chaos. A figure cloaked in radiant white stood at the center of it all, their face obscured but their presence overwhelming. Aria's breath caught as she realized the figure was reaching for her, their hand outstretched in silent command.

"No," she whispered, her voice trembling. "This isn't real. It's not me."

But the vision didn't fade. It pressed harder, sharper, filling her mind with fragments of a story she couldn't piece together. The figure's outstretched hand glowed with the same green light as the fire in the square, and as their fingers brushed against hers, the flames roared higher.

Aria's body convulsed as the burning warmth in her chest surged again, stronger this time. She fell to her knees, her vision snapping back to the present just in time to see the fire in the square erupt in a column of green light that shot into the sky.

The villagers gasped as one, their voices a collective cry of awe and fear. Some fell to the ground, bowing with their foreheads pressed to the dirt. Others reached out toward her, their hands trembling as though they could feel the power radiating from her.

Aria's chest heaved as she struggled to catch her breath. "Torin..." she choked out, her voice barely audible.

He was at her side in an instant, his hand gripping her arm to steady her. "It's the essence," he said, his voice low but urgent. "It's responding to you."

"I didn't do anything!" she whispered harshly. "I don't—this isn't me!"

"It doesn't matter," he said, his eyes scanning the villagers, who were still frozen in their reverent poses. "They think it is."

The elder stepped forward, her hands clasped in front of her chest. She dropped to her knees before Aria, her head bowed deeply. When she spoke, her voice trembled with emotion, and Aria caught only one word: "Seluna."

"No," Aria said, shaking her head. "You're wrong. I'm not—I'm not her."

But her protest was drowned out as the villagers erupted into chants again, their voices rising in a triumphant crescendo. The fire, though calmer now, still burned an unnatural green, its light casting Aria in an otherworldly glow.

Torin's grip tightened on her arm. "It doesn't matter what you think, Aria. To them, you're the Shattered Queen."

Aria stared at him, her mind racing. The heat in her chest had begun to fade, but the weight of the visions—and what they might mean—remained. The villagers' chants grew louder, echoing in her ears, and for the first time, she felt the full weight of what they expected her to be.

And the terrifying possibility that she might not have a choice.

The green flames in the fire pit began to wane, shrinking down until they flickered softly like dying embers. The once-roaring heat gave way to a cool, eerie stillness that settled over the square. Aria knelt on the ground, her chest heaving as she tried to catch her breath. Sweat dripped from her brow, tracing lines through the faint patterns of glowing paint on her skin. The visions still lingered in her mind—shattered crowns, broken worlds, and that faceless figure cloaked in light.

"Seluna," someone whispered, their voice tremulous with awe.

It started as a murmur among the villagers, but soon the word rippled through the crowd, growing louder with each repetition. "Seluna! Seluna!" The chant rose again, reverberating off the surrounding huts and trees.

Aria swallowed hard, her hands trembling as she pressed them into the dirt for balance. She wanted to scream that they were wrong, to tell them this was all some horrible misunderstanding, but the words caught in her throat.

The silver-haired elder stepped forward, her movements slow and deliberate. The reverence in her expression made Aria's stomach twist. The elder raised her hands, palms outward, and the chanting fell to a hush. The only sounds were the crackling of the subdued fire and the faint rustle of leaves in the still air.

The elder's voice was steady as she spoke, her words flowing like a song. Aria couldn't understand the language, but she caught the familiar syllables of "Seluna" and another word that Torin had mentioned earlier: "Shattered." The elder turned to

Aria, bowing deeply before addressing the crowd again. Her tone carried the weight of a declaration, and the villagers gasped in unison.

Torin knelt beside her, his voice low and urgent. "She's proclaiming you as the Shattered Queen reborn. The chosen one sent to fulfill the prophecy."

Aria turned her head sharply toward him, her voice a harsh whisper. "And you're just okay with this? You know it isn't true!"

Torin's jaw tightened. "What I believe doesn't matter right now. What they believe does."

"I can't do this," Aria muttered, her voice cracking. "I'm not who they think I am."

The elder's gaze fixed on Aria, her expression expectant. She held out a hand, beckoning Aria to rise. Torin gave her a slight nudge. "Stand up," he said under his breath. "They need to see you accept it."

Aria hesitated, her legs weak and unsteady as she forced herself to her feet. The elder stepped closer, her lined face softening with what looked like pride. She reached out and lightly touched Aria's shoulder, then gestured toward the crowd. Aria followed her motion and froze.

Every villager was on their knees, their foreheads pressed to the dirt. Children clung to their parents, their wide eyes peeking up at her in awe. Warriors who had led her here with spears now knelt in complete submission. The sight was overwhelming.

"Please," Aria whispered, more to herself than anyone else. "Don't do this."

Torin stood beside her now, his voice quieter but firm. "They've waited for this moment for generations, Aria. They've suffered believing this prophecy would save them. Whether it's true or not doesn't matter anymore. You're their hope."

She turned to him, her eyes blazing with frustration. "I didn't ask for this! I didn't choose to be their hope. I don't even know what this prophecy is supposed to mean!"

Torin's gaze didn't waver. "None of us choose the roles we're given. We just survive them."

The elder spoke again, her voice rising as she addressed the villagers. She gestured to Aria with both hands, her expression solemn. The crowd erupted into cheers, their cries of "Seluna" mingling with the pounding of drums that began once more. Some of the villagers wept openly, while others clasped their hands together in prayer.

Aria's heart sank further with every cheer. She felt the weight of their hope pressing down on her, suffocating her under its crushing force. They had placed everything—every dream, every belief, every shred of faith they had left—on her shoulders. And she didn't believe a single word of it.

The elder turned to her again, bowing deeply before taking her hand and raising it toward the sky. The crowd roared louder, their voices shaking the air around them. Aria's hand trembled in the elder's grip, but she forced herself to stand still, her face a mask of calm even as her mind screamed for an escape.

Torin leaned in close, his voice low enough that only she could hear. "Breathe, Aria. Just breathe. You can do this."

"I don't even know what 'this' is," she replied through clenched teeth. "I don't know how to be what they need me to be."

"Then figure it out," Torin said bluntly. "Because right now, you don't have a choice."

As the villagers began another chant, swaying in unison, Aria's gaze swept over their faces. Their joy, their reverence, their unshakable belief—it should have been uplifting, but all she felt was dread. They believed in her. They trusted her. And she had no idea how to live up to their expectations.

Her hands fell limply to her sides as the elder released her. The villagers began to rise, their cheers softening into murmured prayers and songs. Aria closed her eyes, willing herself to feel something other than fear.

But all she could think of was the vision—the shattered crown, the fractured world, and the glowing figure reaching out to her. For the first time, she wasn't sure if the vision was a warning or a promise.

Chapter 5
Trials in the Jungle

The jungle opened like a curtain, revealing a hidden sanctuary bathed in light. The air shifted as Aria stepped through the dense foliage, a strange calm descending over the space ahead. Before her lay the Mirror Pools—vast, glassy expanses of water nestled in the heart of the jungle. The sunlight filtering through the canopy above struck the surface of the pools, fracturing into iridescent ribbons of color that seemed to dance in time with the faint hum of the jungle.

Aria stopped in her tracks, her breath catching. "Wow," she murmured, her voice barely above a whisper.

Torin emerged from the shadows behind her, his expression as composed as ever. "The Mirror Pools," he said simply, stepping forward. "A nexus of essence magic. The water reflects more than just the world around it."

Aria turned to him, her curiosity burning. "What does it reflect?"

Torin's eyes narrowed slightly, his tone guarded. "Memories. Fears. Visions of what might come. The elders say the pools reveal truths we aren't ready to see."

"Cryptic as always," she muttered, turning back to the shimmering water. The pools seemed impossibly still, as if they held their breath in anticipation of her approach. The pull she felt was undeniable, a soft tug at the edge of her awareness that made her take a step closer.

"Careful," Torin said sharply, his hand darting out to catch her arm. "The waters are unpredictable. They don't respond to everyone the same way."

"I wasn't going to dive in," Aria shot back, though her voice wavered. She glanced down at his hand, still gripping her arm, and raised an eyebrow. "You can let go now."

Torin hesitated, then released her, his expression unreadable. "Just don't forget why we're here."

Aria snorted, crossing her arms. "I'm not likely to forget. The prophecy, the fragments, the fate of the world. It's a little hard to ignore."

"You'd be surprised how often people do," Torin said, his voice quieter now. He stepped past her, his boots crunching softly against the gravel as he moved closer to the pools. "The fragments are said to lie beneath the surface. If the essence recognizes you, it will show you the way."

"Recognizes me?" she repeated, following him reluctantly. "Like it did with the mural?"

"Something like that," Torin replied. He crouched at the edge of the nearest pool, his reflection rippling faintly as he dipped his fingers into the water. "These waters are ancient, tied directly to the flow of essence. They'll test you before they reveal anything."

"Test me how?" Aria asked, her unease growing.

Torin stood, shaking the water from his hand. "That depends on you."

She let out a frustrated sigh, her gaze returning to the pools. The pull was stronger now, a subtle but insistent urge to move closer, to reach out and touch the surface. "You're really bad at making this sound less terrifying."

"It's not my job to comfort you," he said, his tone edged with dry humor.

"Clearly," she muttered, but her focus was already drifting back to the water. The colors within the pools shifted and swirled, forming patterns that seemed just out of reach, like a memory she couldn't quite grasp.

Torin stepped back, his arms crossed. "If you're going to do this, do it now. The longer you hesitate, the harder it will be."

Aria shot him a glare. "You're just full of encouragement, aren't you?"

He didn't reply, his gaze steady as he watched her. For a moment, she considered turning away, refusing to play along with the prophecy's game. But the pull of the pools was too strong, a whisper in her mind that drowned out her doubts.

Taking a deep breath, she knelt at the edge of the largest pool. The water shimmered like liquid glass, its surface cool and inviting. Slowly, she reached out, her fingertips brushing the edge.

A jolt of energy coursed through her hand, not painful but startling. She gasped, pulling back instinctively, but the pull only grew stronger. "What was that?" she asked, her voice tight.

"The pools acknowledging you," Torin said. "You're connected to them now. Keep going."

Aria hesitated, then reached out again. This time, she pressed her palm flat against the water. The surface rippled outward, glowing faintly as the energy spread through her body. Her vision blurred, and for a moment, the jungle around her seemed to fade away.

She was no longer kneeling at the edge of a pool. Instead, she stood in an endless expanse of mirrored water, the sky above a swirling tapestry of light and shadow. The reflection staring back at her wasn't her own—it was the figure from the mural, crowned in jagged crystals and radiating power.

The figure's voice echoed in her mind, soft yet commanding. *You are the bridge. You must choose.*

Aria stumbled back, the vision shattering as her hand slipped from the water. She gasped, her chest heaving as the world snapped back into focus. Torin was at her side in an instant, his expression sharp with concern.

"What did you see?" he asked.

She shook her head, her voice trembling. "I… I don't know. A figure. Light and shadow. It said I have to choose."

Torin's jaw tightened, but he didn't press her further. "The pools don't lie. Whatever it showed you, it's part of your path."

Aria looked back at the water, her reflection rippling faintly. The pull was gone now, replaced by a heavy sense of foreboding. She swallowed hard, her voice barely above a whisper. "What if I make the wrong choice?"

Torin's gaze softened, just enough to surprise her. "Then we'll find another way."

For the first time, his words felt less like a command and more like a promise. It wasn't enough to ease her fear, but it was enough to keep her moving forward.

The Mirror Pools shimmered as if alive, their still surfaces now rippling faintly in response to Aria's presence. The jungle around her seemed to recede, the chirping of insects and rustling of leaves dimming until only the soft hum of the pools remained. She knelt once more at the water's edge, her reflection staring back at her, distorted by the faint waves. Something about the stillness felt unnatural, as if the pools were holding their breath.

Torin stood a few paces behind her, silent and watchful. His presence was steadying, even if his quiet scrutiny set her nerves on edge.

"You're sure this is safe?" she asked, her voice thin but steady.

"As safe as anything in Ilyria," he replied. There was no humor in his tone, just quiet reassurance. "If the essence is responding to you, it's because it wants to."

"That's not exactly comforting," she muttered, but her gaze was already drawn back to the water.

The pull was irresistible now, a subtle yet insistent tug at the edges of her awareness. Slowly, she leaned closer, her breath fogging the mirror-like surface. The colors beneath the water swirled faintly, coalescing into patterns she couldn't quite decipher. She hesitated, then let her hand graze the surface once more.

The moment her skin touched the water, the world shifted.

The jungle vanished, replaced by an endless expanse of silver light. The ground beneath her feet shimmered like liquid metal, and the sky above was a swirling vortex of shadows and pale illumination. It was both vast and claustrophobic, as though she were caught in the heart of something ancient and alive.

"Aria."

The voice came from everywhere and nowhere, soft yet commanding. It wasn't Torin—it was feminine, melodic, and laced with a sorrow that made Aria's chest tighten. She turned, her heart pounding, and froze.

Standing before her was a figure cloaked in radiant light. The woman was tall, her posture regal despite the weight of unseen burdens that seemed to press on her shoulders. Her face was striking, framed by hair that glowed like molten gold. But it was her eyes that held Aria captive—violet and filled with unspoken grief, as though they carried the weight of a thousand lifetimes.

"You're her," Aria whispered. "Maelis."

The figure inclined her head, a silent acknowledgment. She didn't speak, but her gaze was enough to convey her intent. She reached out, her hand glowing faintly as it extended toward Aria.

"I don't understand," Aria said, taking an instinctive step back. "Why me? I'm not you. I can't be."

Maelis didn't respond. Instead, she moved closer, her expression calm but filled with an urgency that sent a shiver down Aria's spine. The light around her seemed to pulse, and for a brief moment, images flashed before Aria's eyes—scenes of battle, of tribes uniting under a single banner, of Maelis standing at the edge of a great chasm, her hands outstretched as glowing fissures split the earth.

Aria stumbled, her breath hitching as the vision faded. "No," she said, shaking her head. "That's not me. I'm not a queen, or a savior, or anything like that."

Maelis stepped closer still, her hand now inches from Aria's. Though she didn't speak, her gaze conveyed a silent plea: *Accept what you are.*

"I can't," Aria said, her voice breaking. "I didn't ask for this."

The sorrow in Maelis's eyes deepened, but she didn't waver. Her hand hovered in the space between them, the light radiating from her growing brighter. Aria could feel its warmth, a gentle yet insistent presence that reached into her very soul.

For a moment, she considered reaching back. But fear held her still.

"I don't even know how," Aria whispered, tears stinging her eyes. "If I fail—if I make the wrong choice—how do I live with that?"

Maelis's expression softened, and for the first time, a faint smile touched her lips. It was bittersweet, filled with a compassion that only deepened Aria's unease. The queen's light pulsed again, then began to fade, her form dissolving into the silvery expanse around them.

"Wait!" Aria called, stepping forward, but the vision dissolved entirely. The ground beneath her feet shifted, and the world snapped back into focus.

She was kneeling by the Mirror Pools again, her reflection rippling faintly in the water. Her breaths came in ragged gasps, and her hands trembled as she braced herself against the ground.

"Aria," Torin's voice broke through her daze, steady but tinged with concern. He crouched beside her, his hand hovering near her shoulder. "What happened?"

She shook her head, unable to meet his gaze. "I saw her," she said hoarsely. "Maelis. She… she wanted me to take her hand."

Torin's jaw tightened, but he didn't press her. "Did you?"

"No," Aria admitted, her voice trembling. "I couldn't."

He was silent for a moment, then said, "The essence shows what we need to see, not what we want to. Whatever she meant, it's part of your path now."

"I don't want this path," she whispered, her eyes fixed on the shimmering pools. "But it won't leave me alone."

Torin's gaze softened, his voice quieter now. "Then don't walk it alone."

She looked at him, her breath still uneven. For the first time, his presence felt less like an obligation and more like an anchor—a lifeline in a world she couldn't yet comprehend.

The jungle seemed to exhale as Aria pulled herself back from the edge of the Mirror Pools, her hands trembling. She felt lightheaded, her body humming with a strange, unfamiliar energy. The once-muted jungle sounds now rushed back in a cascade of vibrant clarity—the chirping of insects, the rustle of leaves, the distant calls of unseen creatures. It was as if the jungle itself was alive in her mind, each sound a part of a larger rhythm she hadn't noticed before.

Torin stepped closer, his eyes sharp as they searched hers. "Aria," he said cautiously, his voice low. "What's happening?"

She opened her mouth to respond but stopped, startled. Her chest swelled with a pulse that wasn't her own, a steady, grounding thrum that seemed to come from everywhere at once. "I... I can feel it," she whispered. "The jungle. It's like it's... breathing."

Torin frowned, his gaze flicking between her and the pools. "What do you mean?"

"I mean—" She stopped again, distracted as the energy pulsed through her, sharper this time. She reached out instinctively, her fingers brushing the leaves of a nearby plant. The moment her skin made contact, the leaves quivered and unfurled as if drawn toward her. "Do you see that?"

Torin's expression tightened, his voice edged with both caution and curiosity. "What did the pools show you?"

"Maelis," she said, her voice distant, her attention still on the plant. "She didn't speak, but it was like she wanted me to feel this. To connect with this." Her hand drifted to another vine, and it, too, responded, curling toward her like a living thread.

"Aria—" Torin began, his tone sharpening.

Before he could finish, a faint glow radiated from beneath her fingertips, spreading out like veins of light through the plant and into the ground. The energy rippled outward, and the jungle responded. Branches shifted, flowers bloomed in fast-forward, and even the air seemed to vibrate with a new vitality.

Torin stepped back slightly, his hand instinctively moving to the hilt of his blade. "The essence," he muttered. "It's reacting to you."

Aria pulled her hand back quickly, her eyes wide. "I didn't mean to do that! It just… happened."

The sound of movement drew both their attention. Figures emerged from the jungle shadows—members of the Verdant Clans, their expressions frozen in awe. One by one, they dropped to their knees, their heads bowed low.

"What are they doing?" Aria asked, panic threading her voice.

"They're kneeling," Torin said simply, his hand falling away from his weapon. His expression was unreadable, though his tone carried an edge of finality. "You've shown them proof."

"Proof?" she echoed, looking between him and the kneeling clanspeople. "Of what?"

"Of the prophecy," Torin replied. He stepped closer, lowering his voice as if to shield the moment from the watching crowd. "They believe you're the Shattered Queen reborn. And now they've seen it for themselves."

"No," Aria said, shaking her head. "This—this doesn't mean anything. I didn't choose this!"

One of the elders stepped forward, her silver hair gleaming in the dim light. She spoke in the lyrical language of the clans, her tone reverent. The words came quickly, as though she were reciting a prayer.

"What's she saying?" Aria whispered to Torin.

"She says the jungle has chosen you," he said, his tone steady but his eyes wary. "That the essence flows through you like it did through Maelis."

Aria's breath hitched, the weight of the elder's words sinking into her. "But I don't even know how I did it! What if it's just a mistake?"

The elder finished speaking and bowed deeply before Aria, her hands pressed to her chest. The rest of the clanspeople echoed the gesture, their whispers blending into a low hum of awe and devotion.

Torin leaned in, his voice quiet but firm. "It's not a mistake. Whatever this is, the essence recognized you. That's not something you can fake."

"I don't want them bowing to me," she said, her voice breaking. "I don't want to be this… this thing they've been waiting for."

Torin straightened, his gaze steady. "It doesn't matter what you want. It matters what they believe. And right now, they believe you're the one who can save them."

Aria closed her eyes, her breathing shallow. The hum of the jungle and the soft whispers of the clanspeople pressed in around her, a chorus she couldn't escape. When she opened her eyes again, Torin was watching her closely, his expression softer than she expected.

"They need hope, Aria," he said quietly. "Whether you want to be their Queen or not, you've already become something to them."

She stared at him, her hands still trembling. "And what if I can't live up to it?"

"Then you'll figure out what you can be," he said simply.

The clanspeople began to rise, their movements slow and reverent. The elder spoke again, her voice lifting in a tone of certainty that made Aria's stomach twist.

"She says the path begins here," Torin translated. His gaze flicked to the jungle around them, then back to her. "Whatever comes next, you don't face it alone."

Aria exhaled shakily, the pulse of the essence still faintly present beneath her skin. She wasn't sure if it comforted her or terrified her. But for now, she nodded, the weight of the moment pressing heavy on her chest.

"Let's go," she said, her voice quiet but firm. And with Torin at her side, she turned away from the pools, her path stretching into the unknown.

The jungle's once-vivid hum seemed distant now, muffled beneath the weight pressing on Aria's chest. The Mirror Pools lay behind her, their shimmering surfaces calm once more, but the energy that had coursed through her remained, a faint echo in her veins. Every step felt heavier as if the jungle itself had placed an invisible yoke around her shoulders.

She stopped walking and sat on a moss-covered rock, letting her head fall into her hands. Her breathing was shallow, uneven. The images from the vision flashed behind her closed eyes—Maelis's sorrowful gaze, the swirling essence, the sense of inevitability that had wrapped around her like a net.

Torin stood a short distance away, watching her in silence. His arms were crossed, his expression unreadable as he leaned against a nearby tree. The faint rustle of leaves above them was the only sound for a long moment.

Finally, Aria broke the silence. "I don't think I can do this," she said, her voice barely above a whisper. Her hands dropped into her lap, and she looked up at him, her eyes clouded with fear and exhaustion. "It's too much. The prophecy, Maelis, the essence—how am I supposed to be all of that?"

Torin didn't move at first. He simply studied her, his dark eyes steady. "You're not supposed to be all of it," he said finally, his tone calm but firm. "You're supposed to be you."

Aria let out a hollow laugh, shaking her head. "That's not what they want. The clans, the elders—they're not looking at me.

They're looking at her. At some ancient queen they think I'm supposed to be."

"They're looking for hope," Torin said, stepping closer. "That doesn't mean you have to be her. It means you have to decide who you are."

She frowned, her gaze dropping to the ground. "What if I'm not enough?"

Torin crouched in front of her, resting his arms on his knees. "You don't have to be enough today. You just have to keep moving forward."

Her throat tightened at his words. "That's easy for you to say. You've been trained for this—fighting, leading, surviving. I was dragged here with no warning and told I'm part of some prophecy I didn't even know existed."

He nodded slowly, his expression softening. "You're right. You weren't prepared for this. But you're here, and that means something."

"What does it mean?" she asked, her voice trembling.

Torin hesitated, his gaze dropping briefly before meeting hers again. "It means the essence chose you. It means there's a reason you're here, even if you don't see it yet."

Aria shook her head, tears pricking at the corners of her eyes. "I didn't ask to be chosen. I just wanted to study history, not… live it."

"That's fair," he said, his voice quiet. "But history doesn't ask for permission."

She let out another laugh, this one tinged with bitterness. "You've got an answer for everything, don't you?"

Torin's lips twitched, almost forming a smile. "Not everything. But enough."

Aria looked away, her gaze drifting back toward the Mirror Pools in the distance. Their calm surfaces seemed so at odds with the storm raging inside her. "What if I mess this up?" she asked after a long pause. "What if I fail, and everything falls apart?"

Torin straightened, his voice steady. "Then we figure it out. Together."

She blinked, surprised by the certainty in his tone. "You really think that's possible?"

"I do," he said simply. "Because you're not alone in this. No matter what the prophecy says, it's not just your burden to carry."

The weight on her chest lifted, just slightly, and she met his gaze again. For the first time, she saw something she hadn't expected: quiet faith. Not in the prophecy or the essence, but in her.

"Thanks," she said softly, her voice barely audible.

Torin inclined his head, stepping back to give her space. "Take a moment. When you're ready, we move forward."

She nodded, her thoughts still spinning but her breathing steadier now. The burden hadn't disappeared, but with Torin's quiet presence beside her, it didn't feel quite so impossible. For the first time, she began to think that maybe, just maybe, she could find a way to carry it.

Chapter 6
Shadows in the Wild

The jungle seemed alive with intent, its dense foliage pressing in from all sides as Aria and Torin made their way along the barely discernible path. Vines hung low from the towering trees, their gnarled roots snaking across the damp ground. Every step Aria took felt precarious, her boots slipping on moss-covered rocks and sinking into the soft earth. The air was thick with moisture, clinging to her skin and making it hard to breathe.

"Watch your footing," Torin said sharply, glancing back at her. "The roots are deceptive. Step wrong, and you'll twist your ankle."

"Thanks," Aria muttered, swatting at an oversized insect buzzing near her face. "I hadn't noticed."

"You're not helping yourself with that attitude," Torin replied, his tone clipped. "You want to survive this jungle? Start listening."

She huffed, brushing a strand of damp hair from her face. "I didn't exactly plan for a crash course in survival. A little patience wouldn't kill you."

Torin stopped abruptly, turning to face her. His broad shoulders seemed even larger in the shadowy light filtering through the canopy. "Patience doesn't keep you alive out here.

Awareness does. If you're too busy complaining to pay attention, you're not going to make it far."

"Wow," Aria shot back, hands on her hips. "Inspiring. Truly."

Torin's expression hardened. "You think this is a joke? The jungle isn't just trees and vines. It's predators, traps, poisonous plants. One mistake, and you're dead."

She rolled her eyes but bit back a retort. Instead, she stepped around him and continued down the path, muttering under her breath. "Great pep talk. Really makes me feel like I belong here."

He let out an exasperated sigh but followed her, keeping a careful eye on their surroundings. The silence between them stretched, broken only by the occasional rustle of leaves or the distant call of an unseen bird.

Aria stumbled again, catching herself on a low-hanging branch. "Okay," she said, her voice tight. "Maybe I could use a few tips."

Torin smirked faintly but didn't comment on her change in tone. Instead, he knelt by a patch of ferns, brushing the dirt away from their base. "These roots," he said, gesturing. "Good for water if you're desperate. Just peel the outer layer and chew. They'll keep you hydrated."

"Chew a root," Aria repeated, raising an eyebrow. "Sounds delicious."

"It's better than dying of thirst," Torin said flatly, standing and brushing dirt from his hands. "And these," he added, pointing to a thick vine curling around a nearby tree, "are essence vines. You see the way they shimmer slightly in the light?"

She squinted at the vine. "Barely."

"That shimmer means they're full of essence energy. Dangerous to touch if you don't know what you're doing. They'll react if you disturb them—lash out."

"Lash out?" she asked, narrowing her eyes. "You're telling me the plants attack people now?"

"They don't attack," Torin corrected. "They protect themselves. There's a difference."

"Sure there is," Aria muttered, stepping wide around the vine as they resumed walking. "This place just keeps getting better."

The path grew narrower, forcing them to walk single file. Aria stumbled over a root again, barely catching herself before falling. Her hands scraped against the rough bark of a tree, and she cursed under her breath.

"Lift your knees higher when you walk," Torin called back to her. "Stop dragging your feet."

"I'm not dragging my feet," she snapped. "This path is practically vertical. Maybe if you slowed down for five seconds—"

A sudden screech tore through the air, cutting her off. Aria froze, her heart pounding as the sound echoed through the jungle. It was sharp and guttural, unlike anything she had ever heard before.

"What was that?" she whispered, her voice tight with fear.

Torin didn't answer immediately. He crouched low, scanning the surrounding trees with his hand on the hilt of his blade. "Probably a jungle hawk," he said finally, though his tone was far from reassuring. "They're territorial but usually stay high in the canopy."

"Usually?" Aria hissed, gripping a nearby branch for support. "What about the times they don't?"

Torin glanced at her, his face serious. "Then we move fast and stay quiet."

"Fantastic," she muttered, her grip tightening as she scanned the trees nervously. "Remind me again why we're out here?"

"Because you need to learn," Torin said simply. "This jungle is unforgiving, Aria. It doesn't care who you are or why you're here. If you want to survive, you have to adapt."

"Adapt," she echoed, shaking her head. "Great. No pressure."

They pressed on, the tension between them easing slightly as the screeching faded into the distance. Torin slowed his pace, occasionally pointing out plants or warning her about hidden dangers. Despite her frustration, Aria found herself paying closer attention, her mind cataloging his advice even as her legs ached from the relentless trek.

The jungle seemed to grow heavier as they continued, the air thickening until it felt like a weight pressing down on her shoulders. The shadows deepened, and the sounds of the jungle shifted—no longer the chaotic hum of life but something quieter, watchful.

Aria glanced around uneasily. "Is it just me, or does it feel like the jungle is… I don't know, watching us?"

Torin didn't look back. "It's not your imagination."

"That's… comforting," she muttered.

"Stay focused," he said, his voice calm but firm. "We still have a long way to go."

Aria sighed, adjusting her pack and squaring her shoulders. The path ahead was treacherous, but for the first time, she realized that Torin's relentless guidance—annoying as it was—might be the only thing keeping her alive.

The jungle seemed to hold its breath. The usual hum of insects and distant bird calls faded, replaced by an unnerving stillness. Aria stopped mid-step, her boots sinking slightly into the damp ground. The hairs on the back of her neck prickled.

"Torin," she said, her voice barely above a whisper. "Do you hear that?"

He held up a hand, signaling for silence. His eyes scanned the dense foliage ahead, his posture rigid and alert. Aria could see the tension in his shoulders, the way his hand rested on the hilt of his blade.

"What is it?" she asked, her voice trembling.

Before he could answer, a deep, guttural growl rumbled through the air, sending a chill racing down her spine. It was close. Too close.

"Get behind me," Torin ordered sharply, unsheathing his blade in one fluid motion.

"What is it?" she repeated, her voice rising. "Torin, what's out there?"

"Just move!" he barked, his eyes locked on the shadows ahead.

Aria didn't argue this time. She scrambled backward, pressing herself against the wide trunk of a tree. Her heart pounded in her chest as the growl came again, louder this time, vibrating through the ground beneath her feet.

A pair of glowing eyes emerged from the shadows, their predatory gleam fixed on Torin. The creature stepped into the faint light filtering through the canopy, and Aria's breath caught. It was massive—easily the size of a horse—with sleek, obsidian fur that shimmered faintly with an iridescent glow. Its feline form was muscular and powerful, its movements fluid as it prowled closer. Razor-sharp claws dug into the earth with each step, and its teeth gleamed as it bared them in a snarl.

Torin didn't flinch. His blade gleamed in the dim light as he held his ground. "Stay still," he said, his voice low but steady. "Don't move. Don't make a sound."

"What is that thing?" Aria whispered, her voice barely audible.

"A shadow panther," Torin replied grimly. "Essence-born. It's hunting."

"Hunting us?" she asked, her voice trembling.

"Most likely," he said, shifting his stance slightly. "They don't hunt for food. They hunt for the kill."

The panther lunged, its massive body a blur of motion. Torin moved just as quickly, sidestepping the attack and bringing his blade down in a sweeping arc. The weapon glanced off the creature's shimmering fur, sparks flying as it snarled in fury and wheeled around for another strike.

"Go!" Torin shouted over his shoulder, his voice fierce. "Run! Now!"

"I'm not leaving you!" Aria yelled back, her voice shaking but firm.

The panther lunged again, its claws slashing through the air. Torin blocked the strike with his blade, the force of the impact driving him back a step. He gritted his teeth and swung again, this time catching the beast's shoulder. It howled, the sound sharp and grating, but it didn't falter.

"Aria!" he shouted, his voice laced with frustration. "You're not helping me by standing there! Move!"

She hesitated, her body frozen in fear and indecision. The panther's glowing eyes flicked toward her, and for a moment, she thought it might come after her instead. But Torin moved to intercept, slashing at its side and drawing its attention back to him.

The creature's movements were relentless, its speed and strength overwhelming. It circled Torin, its tail lashing as it looked for an opening. Torin's breaths came in sharp gasps, sweat dripping down his face as he matched its movements step for step.

"Torin, you can't fight that thing alone!" Aria called out, her voice high with panic.

"Then figure out how to help!" he snapped, his blade clashing against the panther's claws again. "Do something!"

Aria's mind raced, her fear threatening to drown her. She looked around desperately for anything that might help—a weapon, a distraction, anything. Her eyes landed on a thick branch lying nearby, its end jagged and sharp.

"Okay, okay," she muttered to herself, grabbing the branch. It felt heavy in her hands, awkward and unwieldy, but it was better than nothing. She crept forward, her heart pounding in her chest.

The panther lunged again, and this time, Torin stumbled, the force of the attack driving him to one knee. The creature roared, rearing back for a killing blow.

"Hey!" Aria shouted, adrenaline surging as she swung the branch with all her strength. It connected with the panther's flank, the jagged edge digging into its shimmering fur. The beast let out a furious snarl, turning its glowing eyes on her.

"Oh no," she breathed, her grip tightening on the branch.

The panther lunged at her, but Torin was faster. He surged to his feet, driving his blade into the creature's side with a fierce cry. The beast howled, thrashing wildly as it tried to dislodge him. Torin twisted the blade, and the glow in the panther's eyes flickered before it collapsed with a final, guttural growl.

The jungle fell silent again, the tension breaking like a snapped wire. Torin stood over the beast, his chest heaving as he pulled his blade free. Aria dropped the branch, her legs giving out as she sank to the ground.

"Are you okay?" Torin asked, his voice rough but steady as he turned to her.

She nodded weakly, her breath coming in shaky gasps. "I think so. You?"

He wiped the blade on the grass, his expression grim. "I've been better."

Aria managed a weak laugh, though it quickly turned into a sob. "What the hell was that?"

Torin sheathed his blade and offered her a hand, his tone softening. "Welcome to the jungle, Aria. This is just the beginning."

The jungle seemed to close in around Aria, the shadows stretching longer, darker, as though alive with menace. Her back pressed against the wide trunk of a tree, her breaths shallow and rapid. The beast crouched a few yards away, its glowing eyes fixed on her with unrelenting predatory hunger. Each of its movements was slow and deliberate, the panther-like creature savoring the moment before it struck.

Torin was sprawled on the ground several feet away, his blade out of reach. He groaned as he tried to push himself up, his face pale and streaked with dirt and sweat. "Aria," he rasped, his voice strained. "Run."

"I can't!" she shouted, her voice tight with panic. "I—I can't leave you!"

The beast growled low, the sound rumbling through the air like a warning. It crept closer, its claws digging into the soft earth, each step purposeful. The faint shimmer of its fur in the dim light was hypnotic, otherworldly, but Aria's mind raced with fear. There was nowhere to go, no clear escape. The jungle was too dense, the path blocked by roots and foliage.

Her pulse thundered in her ears. Think, Aria. Think. But her thoughts were a jumble of panic and dread.

Torin's voice cut through the chaos. "You need to move! Now!"

"I can't!" she cried again, her back hitting the bark harder as though she could push herself through the tree itself. "I'm trapped!"

The beast snarled, lowering its head as it prepared to lunge. Aria's body went rigid with terror. Her hands clutched at the rough bark behind her, her fingers digging into it. Every instinct screamed at her to run, but her legs refused to move.

And then she felt it.

A strange warmth unfurled in her chest, a pulse of energy that wasn't her own but felt deeply familiar. It spread through her arms, down to her fingertips, a sensation like static crawling beneath her skin. The jungle around her seemed to shift, the shadows trembling, the air heavy with something… alive.

Her breath caught. The warmth grew stronger, more insistent, pulling her toward something she couldn't see but could feel—deep in the earth beneath her feet. She didn't understand it, didn't know what it was, but it was as if the jungle itself was waiting for her command.

The beast tensed, its glowing eyes narrowing as it leapt toward her. Aria's scream tore from her throat as she threw her hands out in desperation. "Stop!"

The ground erupted.

Thick, gnarled vines shot up from the earth, twisting and coiling with a life of their own. They surged toward the beast, wrapping around its legs and body with a force that sent it crashing to the ground mid-leap. The creature roared, thrashing wildly as the vines tightened, their sharp thorns digging into its shimmering fur.

Aria stared in shock, her hands still outstretched. The warmth in her chest pulsed stronger, more chaotic now, as though it were feeding the vines directly. Her arms trembled, the sensation almost too much to bear. She had no idea how she was doing this—or how to stop it.

The beast roared again, snapping at the vines with its powerful jaws. The jungle around them seemed to shudder in response, the trees swaying despite the still air. Aria's knees buckled, but she held her ground, her focus locked on the creature. The vines writhed, tightening their grip, but the panther's strength was immense. Slowly, it began to tear free, ripping through the tangled mass with furious determination.

"Aria!" Torin's voice was sharper now, cutting through the haze of power coursing through her. "Let it go! You can't hold it forever!"

"I don't know how!" she shouted, her voice shaking. The warmth in her chest was becoming a burning heat, almost unbearable, as though it would consume her entirely. "I don't know what I'm doing!"

"Breathe," Torin said, his tone softer but urgent. "Focus. You're in control—don't let it take over."

Her breaths came fast and shallow, her vision blurring as the vines thrashed wildly. The beast snarled one last time, its glowing eyes locking onto hers, and then it tore itself free. With a final, guttural growl, it turned and bolted into the shadows, its sleek form disappearing into the dense foliage.

The vines collapsed, slithering back into the earth as though they had never been there. Aria fell to her knees, her chest heaving as the burning heat faded into a dull, aching warmth. She stared at her trembling hands, the reality of what had just happened crashing over her.

"What… what was that?" she whispered, her voice barely audible.

Torin staggered to his feet, his movements slow and pained as he approached her. "That," he said, his voice low, "was essence magic."

Her head snapped up, her eyes wide. "Magic? I—I can't use magic. That's not possible."

"Clearly, it is," Torin replied, his tone grim. "You just did."

She shook her head, her hands trembling as she clenched them into fists. "I didn't mean to. I didn't even know I could."

Torin crouched beside her, his dark eyes searching hers. "It doesn't matter if you meant to or not. The jungle answered you. That kind of power… it doesn't come from nowhere."

Aria looked at him, her breath still uneven. "What does that mean?"

"It means," he said, helping her to her feet, "you're connected to this place. To the essence. Whether you want to be or not."

Her legs wobbled as she stood, the weight of his words sinking in. The jungle was quiet again, but it didn't feel still. It felt alive, watchful, as though waiting for her next move. And for the first time, Aria realized just how little control she had over what lay ahead.

The jungle had fallen unnaturally silent. Not a single bird call or rustle of leaves broke the stillness, as though the world itself held its breath. Aria dropped to her knees, her chest heaving as sweat dripped down her face. The cool, damp earth pressed against her palms, grounding her in the reality of what had just happened. She stared blankly at the spot where the beast had vanished, her heart still hammering in her chest.

"Aria," Torin called softly from behind her. His voice was cautious, uncertain, as though he were speaking to a fragile creature that might break under the weight of his words.

She didn't respond. Her gaze remained fixed on the shadows ahead, her mind racing. She flexed her fingers, the memory of the raw power that had surged through her still tingling in her palms. It had been wild, uncontrollable, like holding a thunderstorm in her hands. She wasn't sure if it had come from her or something else entirely.

Torin moved closer, his boots crunching softly against the dirt. He crouched beside her, his expression unreadable but his tone steady. "That wasn't luck."

Her head jerked toward him, her eyes wide. "What?"

"What you did," he said, his gaze intense, "that was essence magic. Pure, untrained, and dangerous as hell—but magic, nonetheless."

"No," she said quickly, shaking her head as her voice trembled. "No, it wasn't. I—I don't have magic. That's not possible."

Torin raised an eyebrow, his skepticism plain. "You're seriously going to argue with me after what I just saw?"

"It wasn't me!" she snapped, her voice rising. "It was… I don't know, the jungle, or—or the essence, or something else! But it wasn't me."

He let out a low sigh, his patience clearly thinning. "Aria, vines don't just erupt out of the ground on their own. They responded to you. You called them."

"I didn't call anything!" she shot back, her hands clenching into fists. "I don't even know how to do that!"

"And yet you did." Torin's tone was calm but unrelenting. "You can deny it all you want, but I saw it. You felt it."

She opened her mouth to argue but closed it again, her words caught in her throat. Her hands were still trembling, betraying the storm of emotions she was trying to contain. She wanted to scream at him, to push back against his certainty, but deep down, she couldn't ignore the truth. She had felt it—the warmth, the pull, the connection to something far larger than herself.

"It doesn't mean anything," she muttered, her voice quieter now. "It was a fluke. A reaction. Nothing more."

Torin tilted his head, studying her carefully. "A fluke doesn't save your life. It doesn't stop a shadow panther in its tracks."

She looked away, her gaze dropping to the ground. Her fingers dug into the dirt, as though clinging to the earth might anchor her against the weight of his words. "I don't want it to mean anything."

Torin's voice softened slightly, though it carried an edge of urgency. "You don't get to choose what this means, Aria. The jungle doesn't just respond to anyone. The essence… it's tied to you. Whether you want it or not."

She shook her head again, her movements frantic. "No. You're wrong. I'm not—I'm not part of this prophecy. I'm not

Seluna's chosen or the Shattered Queen or whatever they think I am."

"And yet here you are," Torin said pointedly. "Here you are, alive, because the essence chose to answer you."

She met his gaze, her eyes blazing with frustration and fear. "You think I wanted this? That I wanted to be dragged into some prophecy I don't even understand? I didn't ask for any of this!"

"No one asks for it," Torin said evenly. "But it doesn't change the fact that it's happening. You can deny it all you want, but the jungle doesn't lie, Aria. It answered you for a reason."

She fell silent, her chest tight with the weight of his words. The reality of what had happened hung between them, undeniable and terrifying. The jungle had responded to her, had unleashed its power at her command, even if she hadn't meant to. But why? What reason could there possibly be for her to be tied to this world and its magic?

Torin stood slowly, his movements deliberate as he extended a hand to her. "You can spend the rest of the journey denying it, but it won't change what you are. And it won't stop what's coming."

Her breath caught at the ominous note in his voice. She stared at his hand, hesitant, before finally reaching out and letting him pull her to her feet. Her legs felt shaky beneath her, and her palms were still coated in dirt, but she steadied herself with a deep breath.

"I don't know what I am," she admitted quietly, her voice barely audible. "But I know what I'm not. I'm not the Shattered Queen."

Torin's lips pressed into a thin line. "We'll see," he said simply, his tone unreadable.

They began walking again, the silence of the jungle pressing down on them once more. But this time, the quiet didn't feel empty. It felt alive, watchful, as though the world itself had shifted and was waiting for her next move. And deep down, Aria couldn't help but wonder if Torin was right.

Chapter 7
Fractured Memories

The campfire had long since burned low, its embers glowing faintly in the cool night air. The jungle around them was alive with the soft hum of nocturnal creatures, but for Aria, the sounds were distant, muffled by the weight of her own thoughts. She lay on her back, staring up at the dark canopy overhead, her mind replaying the messenger's words: *Turn back, girl, or you will see Ilyria consumed by the void.*

Despite her resolve earlier in the day, the memory of those glowing red eyes gnawed at her, burrowing into her thoughts like a splinter she couldn't remove. She closed her eyes, willing herself to sleep, but when it came, it brought no peace.

She stood in a void, an endless expanse of darkness punctuated by faint glimmers of light that flickered like dying stars. The air was thick, suffocating, and the silence was absolute. She turned in slow circles, searching for something—anything—but the emptiness stretched endlessly in every direction.

"Aria."

The voice was soft, almost tender, but it carried an edge that made her blood run cold. She spun toward the sound, and there he was. Not the messenger this time, but something far worse.

Morvan.

He emerged from the shadows, his form indistinct but menacing. His eyes burned with the same crimson fire as the messenger's, but they were sharper, more alive. His presence filled the void, pressing down on her like a weight she couldn't escape.

"You walk a path you cannot hope to finish," he said, his voice a low, hypnotic murmur. "This world will break you before it lets you save it."

Aria tried to speak, but her voice caught in her throat. She wanted to shout at him, to tell him he was wrong, but the words wouldn't come.

"You are nothing but a spark," Morvan continued, stepping closer. "And I will snuff you out."

The shadows around him twisted, reaching for her like living tendrils. She stumbled back, her chest tightening as the darkness closed in. But then, from somewhere deep within her, a light flickered. It was faint, a tiny flame, but it pushed back against the encroaching void.

Morvan paused, his burning eyes narrowing. "You think that will save you?" he hissed. "The essence cannot shield you from me. It is mine to command."

The flame inside her flared brighter, defiant. She clenched her fists, her fear giving way to anger. "You're wrong," she said, her voice steady now. "It's not yours. And I won't let you win."

Morvan laughed, a low, bone-chilling sound. "We shall see, little queen."

The shadows surged forward, swallowing her whole.

Aria jerked awake with a gasp, her chest heaving as if she'd been underwater. The jungle was still dark, the fire reduced to faint embers. She pressed a hand to her chest, feeling the rapid beat of her heart as she tried to steady her breathing.

"Another nightmare?" Torin's voice broke the silence.

She turned her head and saw him sitting nearby, his silhouette barely visible in the dim light. His blade rested across his lap, his posture relaxed but alert, as though he'd been watching over her.

Aria sat up, pulling her knees to her chest. "Yeah," she said quietly. "It was… worse this time."

"Morvan," he guessed, his tone even.

She nodded, staring into the faint glow of the fire. "He was there. Not just his messenger. Him."

Torin leaned forward slightly, his gaze sharp despite the low light. "What did he say?"

She hesitated, the memory of the dream still raw. "That I can't finish this. That the world will break me before I save it."

Torin's jaw tightened, and for a moment, he didn't speak. Then he said, "He wants you to believe that."

"Well, it's working," she muttered, burying her face in her hands. "I don't even know how to fight something like him."

"You don't fight him yet," Torin said, his voice firm but not unkind. "You focus on what's in front of you. One step at a time."

Aria looked up, her voice trembling. "It's not just fear. It's… I don't know if I'm enough."

Torin's gaze softened, and he shifted closer. "Fear's normal. Doubt's normal. What matters is what you do with them."

She let out a slow, shaky breath. "And what do I do?"

"Keep moving," he said simply. "You don't have to win today. Just don't stop."

She nodded, his words settling over her like a fragile shield. "Thanks," she said softly.

Torin stood, his blade catching a faint glint of moonlight as he moved toward the edge of the camp. "Get some rest," he said over his shoulder. "We leave at dawn."

She watched him disappear into the shadows, his presence a steady anchor in the storm of her thoughts. The jungle around her seemed darker now, more alive, but she refused to let the fear consume her. She wasn't ready to face Morvan yet, but when the time came, she would be. She had to be.

The jungle gave way to a small clearing, its center dominated by a thatched hut woven seamlessly into the surrounding trees.

Herbs hung from the eaves, their earthy scents mixing with the damp air. Aria followed Torin into the clearing, her gaze darting around, taking in the signs of life—a small garden, jars filled with brightly colored powders, and the faint glow of runes carved into the stones that lined the path.

"She's here," Torin said, his tone curt.

"Who is she exactly?" Aria asked, keeping her voice low. "You've been pretty vague."

Torin glanced at her, his jaw tightening. "She's my sister."

Aria blinked. "Wait, what? You have a sister? You didn't think to mention that earlier?"

Before Torin could respond, the door to the hut creaked open, and a woman stepped into the clearing. She was tall and willowy, with piercing green eyes that locked onto Aria with unnerving intensity. Her auburn hair was tied back in an intricate braid, and she wore simple, flowing garments that seemed at odds with the sharpness of her gaze.

"Torin," the woman said, her voice smooth but laced with something unreadable. "I wondered when you'd come crawling back."

"Eira," Torin replied, his tone clipped. "We need your help."

Eira's eyes flicked to Aria, narrowing slightly. "And who's this?" she asked, though her tone suggested she already knew the answer.

"I'm Aria," she said, stepping forward. "And I'm guessing you're Eira?"

"Perceptive," Eira said with a faint smirk. Her gaze lingered on Aria for a moment before returning to Torin. "You've been busy, haven't you?"

"This isn't about me," Torin said, his voice firm. "It's about her. We're on a mission, and we need supplies."

"Supplies," Eira repeated, tilting her head. "Of course. But you don't just show up after years of silence for supplies, Torin. What's really going on?"

Torin's jaw tightened, but he didn't look away. "I don't have time for this, Eira. Will you help us or not?"

Eira let out a soft laugh, crossing her arms. "You haven't changed a bit. Still barking orders, still expecting everyone to fall in line."

"I'm not here to argue," Torin said, his tone dangerously calm. "We're trying to stop Morvan."

The mention of the dark sorcerer wiped the amusement from Eira's face. She studied him for a long moment before her gaze shifted back to Aria. "And she's the one everyone's talking about? The Shattered Queen reborn?"

"I'm standing right here," Aria said, folding her arms. "And yes, apparently that's me."

Eira's lips quirked into a faint smile, but it didn't reach her eyes. "I see. The essence chose you, did it?"

"I guess," Aria said, her voice tinged with irritation. "Not that I had much of a say in it."

"Interesting," Eira murmured, her gaze flickering to Torin. "And you're just… following her? After everything?"

Torin's eyes narrowed. "This isn't about us."

"Isn't it?" Eira asked, her tone light but cutting. "I remember when you used to question orders, Torin. When you didn't blindly follow anyone."

"I'm not blindly following," he said sharply. "I'm doing what needs to be done."

Eira's smirk returned, but it was sharper now, almost predatory. "Of course you are. How noble."

Aria shifted uncomfortably, sensing the tension between them. "Look," she said, stepping forward, "we don't have time for this. If you can help us, great. If not, we'll figure it out on our own."

Eira turned her piercing gaze on Aria again, her expression unreadable. "You've got some fire, I'll give you that," she said. "But fire doesn't last long in a storm."

"Maybe not," Aria said evenly. "But it's better than sitting in the dark."

For a moment, Eira said nothing, her gaze locked on Aria's. Then, to Aria's surprise, she let out a soft laugh. "I like her," Eira said, glancing at Torin. "She's got more spine than you."

"Eira," Torin warned.

"Relax, little brother," she said, holding up her hands. "I'll help you. For now. But don't expect me to fall in line like the rest of your followers."

"Eira—" Torin started, but she cut him off with a wave of her hand.

"Save it," she said. "Let me gather what you need."

She turned and disappeared into the hut, leaving Aria and Torin alone in the clearing. Aria looked at him, raising an eyebrow. "Well, that was... intense."

"She's always been like this," Torin said, his voice tight. "Don't let her get under your skin."

"Funny," Aria said with a faint smirk. "I could say the same about you."

Torin gave her a sharp look but didn't respond. Instead, his gaze lingered on the door to the hut, a flicker of unease crossing his face. Aria didn't push him, but she filed the moment away, sensing there was more to the story than he was letting on.

The jungle felt unnaturally still as Aria followed Eira along a narrow path lined with twisted vines and towering trees. The thick canopy above allowed only slivers of moonlight to pierce through, casting the world in silvery shadows. Torin was a few paces behind, his footsteps muffled by the dense underbrush. The tension between the siblings was palpable, hanging in the air like a storm about to break.

"How much farther?" Aria asked, her voice low but laced with impatience.

"Not far," Eira replied over her shoulder, her tone light. Too light. "I told you, there's an ancient nexus ahead. The essence flows strongest there. If you're truly connected to it, you'll feel it."

Torin's voice cut through the night, sharp and skeptical. "You never mentioned a nexus before."

Eira turned slightly, her green eyes gleaming in the faint light. "You never asked."

Aria glanced back at Torin, her unease growing. His hand rested on the hilt of his blade, and his gaze was fixed on Eira with a suspicion that mirrored the knot tightening in Aria's stomach.

"Eira," Torin said, his tone dangerously calm. "Why are you really helping us?"

Eira laughed softly, shaking her head. "Always so mistrustful, little brother. Not everyone has ulterior motives."

"Not everyone," Torin agreed. "But you do."

Before Eira could respond, Aria stopped abruptly. Something about the clearing ahead felt wrong. The trees were twisted unnaturally, their branches clawing at the sky like skeletal fingers. The air was colder, heavier, and the faint hum of the essence that usually calmed her was absent.

"Eira," Aria said slowly, her voice wary. "What is this place?"

"The nexus," Eira said, her smile sharp and unsettling. "Or at least, it will be—for him."

Aria's blood ran cold. "For who?"

A low, sinister chuckle echoed from the shadows, and Aria's heart sank. The air shifted, and dark figures began to emerge from the trees, their eyes glowing with an unnatural crimson light. Cloaked in shadow, they carried wicked blades and moved with eerie precision, surrounding the trio in a tight circle.

"Morvan's forces," Torin spat, drawing his blade in a single fluid motion. "Eira, what have you done?"

Eira stepped back, her smile fading as her expression hardened. "I've done what needed to be done," she said, her voice cold. "You've always been so blind, Torin. Following the prophecy, following her—" She gestured toward Aria. "But Morvan offers something real. Power. Safety. And I intend to survive."

"By selling us out?" Torin growled, his blade gleaming in the moonlight.

"You wouldn't understand," Eira said, her tone sharp. "You've always clung to your precious honor, no matter the cost. But honor won't save you now."

Aria's voice trembled with anger. "You brought us here to die."

"No," Eira said, her expression unreadable. "I brought you here to choose. Surrender, and Morvan might spare you. Fight, and you'll only delay the inevitable."

"I'll take my chances," Aria said, her fists clenched.

The shadowed warriors closed in, their movements silent and deliberate. Torin stepped in front of Aria, his stance protective. "Stay behind me," he said, his voice low but firm.

"No," Aria said, her resolve hardening. "I'm not hiding. Not anymore."

Torin didn't argue, his blade flashing as the first warrior lunged. The clash of steel echoed through the clearing, breaking the oppressive silence. Aria reached for the essence, her connection faltering at first but then flaring to life as vines erupted from the ground, tangling the legs of an approaching attacker.

"Aria, move!" Torin shouted, slicing through another foe.

She ducked as a blade swung past her head, adrenaline surging as she focused on the vines, tightening their grip around her enemy. Another attacker charged, but Torin intercepted, his movements swift and precise.

"Eira!" Torin shouted, his voice filled with fury. "Call them off!"

Eira stood at the edge of the clearing, watching with cold detachment. "It's out of my hands now," she said, her tone devoid of remorse. "You made your choice. Now you'll live—or die—with it."

Aria's anger boiled over, and a pulse of essence magic erupted from her hands, sending two of the shadowed warriors flying. "You think Morvan cares about you?" she yelled at Eira. "You're just a pawn to him!"

Eira's smirk faltered, but she quickly regained her composure. "Better a pawn than a martyr."

Before Aria could respond, Torin grabbed her arm. "We need to go. Now."

She hesitated, glancing at Eira one last time. The betrayal cut deep, but the fight wasn't over yet. With a nod, she followed Torin, the two of them cutting a path through the remaining attackers and disappearing into the dense jungle.

The sounds of pursuit faded as they ran, their breaths ragged and their steps frantic. Finally, they stopped, leaning against the thick trunk of a tree. Torin turned to her, his expression grim.

"You okay?" he asked.

"Define okay," Aria said, her voice shaking. "Your sister just tried to feed us to Morvan's goons."

Torin's jaw tightened, but he didn't respond. Instead, he looked back in the direction of the clearing, his eyes dark with anger and something else—pain.

"She made her choice," he said finally, his voice cold. "Now we make ours."

Aria nodded, the sting of Eira's betrayal still fresh but her resolve hardening. "Then we keep going," she said. "No matter what."

The jungle seemed to close in around them, every shadow twisting into something threatening. Aria's breath came in sharp bursts as she ran, her boots slipping on the damp undergrowth. Torin was just ahead, moving with the precision of someone who knew the terrain instinctively, his blade still drawn and gleaming faintly in the dim moonlight filtering through the canopy above.

"Keep moving," he called back over his shoulder, his voice steady despite their frantic pace.

"I'm trying!" Aria snapped, ducking under a low-hanging branch. Her legs ached, and her chest burned, but she forced herself to keep up. The sound of pursuit had faded, but the weight of what they'd left behind clung to her like a second skin.

Finally, Torin slowed, gesturing for her to stop. He crouched low, motioning for her to do the same as he scanned the surrounding jungle. Aria collapsed onto a patch of moss, her chest heaving as she tried to catch her breath.

"Do you think they're still following us?" she asked, her voice barely above a whisper.

Torin shook his head, his gaze fixed on the shadows. "Not yet. Morvan's forces don't stray far from their nexus points. But we're not safe."

"Great," she muttered, pressing the heels of her hands into her eyes. "Because this day wasn't bad enough already."

Torin turned to her, his expression unreadable. "You're not hurt?"

"Just my pride," she said bitterly. "Eira really played me, didn't she?"

Torin's jaw tightened, and he looked away. "She played us both."

Aria studied him for a moment, the sharp lines of his face illuminated by a shaft of moonlight. There was anger there, sure, but something else too—pain. "She's your sister," she said softly. "I can't imagine what that feels like."

He let out a humorless laugh, shaking his head. "Don't waste your sympathy on her. Eira made her choice a long time ago."

"But she's still family," Aria pressed. "That has to mean something."

Torin's gaze snapped back to her, his eyes hard. "Not when she puts the people I care about in danger."

Aria blinked, startled. "You… care about me?"

He frowned, as if the admission had slipped out by accident. "You're part of this now," he said gruffly. "It's my job to keep you alive."

"That's not the same thing," she said, narrowing her eyes. "You didn't have to come after me back there. You could've let them take me."

Torin sighed, running a hand through his hair. "You're not just some burden I'm carrying, Aria. Whether you believe it or not, you're important. To the clans, to the prophecy…" His voice softened, and he looked at her more intently. "To me."

Her breath caught, but she covered it with a laugh. "Well, that's… unexpected. But thanks, I guess."

Torin smirked faintly. "Don't let it go to your head."

They fell into silence, the tension between them easing slightly as the adrenaline of their escape began to fade. The jungle around them was eerily quiet, the only sounds the rustling of leaves and the distant call of an unseen bird.

After a while, Aria spoke again, her voice tentative. "Do you ever think about walking away? Just… leaving all of this behind?"

"Every day," Torin admitted without hesitation. "But walking away doesn't change what's coming. It just makes it someone else's problem."

Aria nodded, her fingers idly tracing patterns in the dirt. "I keep thinking about what Eira said. About Morvan offering safety, power… It's tempting, you know? The idea of not having to fight anymore."

"Tempting doesn't mean right," Torin said firmly. "Morvan's safety is a lie, and his power comes at a cost. You saw what happened back there. Eira's betrayal wasn't about survival—it was about control."

"And you think I'm different?" she asked, meeting his gaze. "That I can do what she couldn't?"

"I think you're stronger than you give yourself credit for," he said, his tone steady. "You're still here, aren't you?"

"Barely," she muttered, but a small smile tugged at her lips despite herself. "You're not bad at this whole pep talk thing."

"Don't get used to it," Torin said, standing and offering her a hand. "We should keep moving."

She hesitated, then took his hand, his grip firm and grounding. As he pulled her to her feet, she felt a flicker of something she hadn't expected—trust. In this hostile, unpredictable world, Torin was the one constant she could rely on.

"Thanks," she said quietly, brushing dirt from her clothes.

He nodded, releasing her hand. "Let's go."

They set off again, the jungle swallowing them in its shadows. The betrayal still stung, and the danger hadn't passed, but for the first time, Aria felt a glimmer of hope. Whatever lay ahead, she wasn't facing it alone. And that, she realized, was enough to keep her going.

Chapter 8
Secrets of the Past

The dense jungle suddenly gave way to a clearing, and Aria froze mid-step, her breath catching as she took in the sight before her. Massive stone pillars, cracked and worn by centuries of erosion, jutted out from the earth like the broken ribs of some long-dead giant. Vines and moss draped over the ancient ruins, their green tendrils softening the jagged edges of the collapsed walls. The air seemed heavier here, charged with a strange, almost reverent energy.

"Is this it?" Aria asked, her voice barely above a whisper.

Torin stopped beside her, his eyes scanning the ruins with practiced caution. His hand instinctively rested on the hilt of his blade as if the stones themselves might spring to life. "The ruins of Talrin," he confirmed. "Or what's left of them."

She stepped forward, her boots crunching softly on the overgrown path. Her fingers brushed against one of the stone pillars, tracing the faded carvings etched into its surface. The intricate patterns seemed to glow faintly in the dappled sunlight filtering through the canopy above.

"These carvings…" Aria murmured, her historian instincts flaring to life. "They're extraordinary. Look at the detail—the symmetry. Whoever made this had to be a master craftsman."

Torin raised an eyebrow but didn't respond immediately. Instead, he moved closer to the base of the largest structure, his gaze sweeping the area for any signs of danger. "Focus, Aria. This place might look abandoned, but that doesn't mean it's safe."

She barely heard him, her attention riveted on the carvings. One particular panel caught her eye—a figure standing at the center of a fractured landscape. The figure's form was imposing, their arms outstretched as if commanding the chaos around them. Jagged lines radiated from their hands, cutting through mountains and rivers alike.

"What's this?" she asked, stepping closer and running her hand gently over the weathered stone.

Torin joined her, his brow furrowing as he studied the image. "It looks like… essence magic."

"More than that," Aria said, shaking her head. "Look at the way the landscape is breaking apart. It's almost like…" Her voice trailed off as a chill ran down her spine. "Like the world itself is shattering."

Torin frowned, his gaze narrowing. "It could be a depiction of the prophecy. The Shattered Queen."

She turned to him, her expression skeptical. "Every time something strange happens, it's tied to that prophecy, isn't it?"

"Because it is," Torin replied evenly. "This ruin, these carvings—they were left behind for a reason. They're warnings, Aria. Pieces of a puzzle."

"Well, it's a pretty cryptic puzzle," she muttered, crossing her arms. "Do you have any idea what it's actually saying?"

Torin gestured to the figure. "That's supposed to be the Queen—Seluna's chosen. She wields the essence to restore balance. Or destroy it, depending on how the prophecy is fulfilled."

Aria scoffed, stepping back from the panel. "That's comforting. No pressure at all."

Torin's jaw tightened, but he didn't rise to the bait. "You're part of this whether you want to be or not. The sooner you accept that, the better."

She threw up her hands. "Great. Another pep talk about destiny. Just what I needed."

He sighed, pinching the bridge of his nose. "Aria, this isn't about what you want. It's about what's happening. Look around you. This ruin, the carvings, everything—it's tied to the essence. To you."

She opened her mouth to argue but stopped herself, her gaze drifting back to the figure on the panel. The power it seemed to exude was palpable, even in stone. For a moment, she imagined herself in that position—standing at the center of chaos, commanding forces she didn't understand.

Her voice was softer when she spoke again. "What if I can't do it? What if I'm not who they think I am?"

Torin's expression softened slightly, though his tone remained firm. "Then you figure it out. Because whether or not you believe in the prophecy, the rifts are real. The danger is real. And we don't have the luxury of waiting for you to come around."

She frowned, her hands clenching at her sides. "You're really terrible at motivational speeches, you know that?"

Torin allowed a faint smirk. "Not my specialty."

They stood in silence for a moment, the weight of the ruins pressing down on them. The air seemed to hum faintly, a reminder that this place was not entirely abandoned. Aria turned away from the carving, her mind buzzing with questions she didn't know how to answer.

"Let's keep moving," she said finally, her voice steady. "If this place is tied to the prophecy, there's got to be more to it."

Torin nodded, his hand tightening on his blade. "Stay close. And keep your eyes open."

As they ventured deeper into the ruins, Aria couldn't shake the feeling that they were being watched. The jungle had an uncanny way of hiding its secrets, and she wasn't sure if the weight in her chest was dread or the pull of something greater waiting to be discovered.

The air inside the ruins grew cooler as they moved deeper into the shadows. The light filtering through the overgrown canopy above seemed to struggle to penetrate the space, leaving jagged shards of sunlight that highlighted patches of moss and vines on the ancient stone. The oppressive silence, broken only by the occasional rustle of leaves or the drip of water, seemed to magnify every sound Aria and Torin made.

"Stay close," Torin said, his voice low but firm. He paused, glancing over his shoulder at Aria. "And watch where you step. The ancient protectors didn't just build for beauty. They built to keep people out."

"Traps?" Aria asked, her tone cautious but curious.

"Plenty," Torin replied, scanning the area ahead. "And they weren't designed to scare intruders. They were designed to kill them."

Aria swallowed hard, her eyes darting to the ground. The thought of deadly traps didn't exactly help the tension knotting in her shoulders. "Good to know," she muttered. "I'll keep that in mind."

Torin gave her a look but didn't respond, his focus shifting back to the path ahead. He crouched low, studying a section of the floor where the moss seemed thinner, revealing faint grooves carved into the stone.

"Pressure plates," he murmured, motioning for her to stop. "Step on the wrong one, and the whole place could come down on us."

"Fantastic," Aria said under her breath, leaning closer. Her eyes narrowed as she studied the grooves. "Wait—those patterns. They're not random."

Torin looked at her, his brow furrowed. "What are you talking about?"

"The carvings," she said, pointing to the faint symbols etched along the edges of the grooves. "They're similar to the ones we saw on the pillars outside. Look—this one here is a marker for safe passage. It's faint, but it's there."

He followed her gaze, his lips pressing into a thin line. "You're sure?"

"As sure as I can be without stepping on it myself," she replied, straightening up. "This isn't my first ancient ruin, you know."

Torin didn't seem convinced, but he nodded. "All right. You lead."

"Wait, me?" she asked, blinking. "A second ago, you were telling me to stay close and not touch anything."

"That was before you decided to start decoding ancient symbols," he said dryly. "If you're so confident, then lead."

She muttered something under her breath but moved forward cautiously, her eyes scanning the floor as she stepped around the grooves. Her historian instincts kicked in, her mind piecing together the patterns and their likely meanings. The symbols weren't just decorative—they were guides, left behind to navigate the treacherous passages.

"This one's safe," she said, pointing to a faint spiral etched into the stone. "And that one over there—don't step on it. The lines are too sharp. It's meant to trigger something."

Torin followed closely, his movements deliberate as he stepped where she indicated. "You're good at this," he admitted grudgingly.

"I spent years studying ancient civilizations," she replied, her voice quieter now. "But I've never seen anything like this before. It's... intricate. Like the traps themselves are part of the art."

"Art that kills," Torin muttered, shaking his head. "Not exactly my style."

She glanced back at him, a faint smile tugging at her lips despite the tension. "You're just not refined enough to appreciate it."

"Refined doesn't keep you alive," he shot back.

The faint banter eased some of the weight in the air, but it was short-lived. As they moved deeper into the ruins, the path narrowed, the carvings growing more elaborate. The air felt colder here, almost damp, and a faint metallic tang lingered on the breeze.

"Careful," Torin said, his voice cutting through the quiet. "Something's off."

Before Aria could respond, her foot caught the edge of a raised stone. She froze, her breath catching as a low rumble echoed through the chamber. The faint sound of grinding stone followed, and she looked down to see the panel she had stepped on sinking slowly into the ground.

"Oh no," she whispered, her voice trembling.

Torin was already moving. He grabbed her arm and yanked her back just as the stone beneath her gave way entirely, revealing a jagged pit lined with sharp, rusted spikes. The sound of the trap activating reverberated through the ruins, and the silence that followed was deafening.

Aria stumbled into Torin, her heart pounding as she stared at the now-exposed pit. "That was—oh my God—I almost—"

"Breathe," Torin said sharply, his grip on her arm steady. "You're fine. But we need to move. Now."

She nodded quickly, her legs shaky as she stepped around the edge of the pit. "I thought... I thought I had it figured out."

"You did," Torin said, his tone softening slightly. "But these traps are meant to trick you. Even the symbols can lie."

Aria exhaled shakily, her gaze lingering on the pit. "Thanks for... you know. Saving me."

"Don't make a habit of it," he replied, his expression hardening again. "I'm not here to babysit you."

"Noted," she said, though her voice was still unsteady. She took another careful step forward, her focus sharpening. "Let's just... get through this."

Torin nodded, his gaze flicking between the floor and the walls. "Stay close. And this time, don't overthink it."

As they continued deeper into the ruins, the weight of their surroundings pressed heavier on Aria. The traps, the carvings, the faint hum of energy in the air—it all felt like a test, as though the ruins themselves were watching, waiting to see if they were worthy of what lay ahead.

The chamber was vast, its domed ceiling lost in shadows. Columns lined the walls, their surfaces carved with intricate depictions of battles and celestial events. At the center of the room stood a pedestal, its edges worn smooth by time. Resting atop it was a shard of crystal, pulsating faintly with a soft, otherworldly light that bathed the chamber in shifting hues of blue and gold.

Aria's breath hitched as she stepped forward, her boots echoing against the stone floor. "That has to be it," she whispered, her voice tinged with awe.

Torin stayed close behind, his gaze sweeping the chamber for any signs of danger. His hand instinctively rested on the hilt of his blade as if the stones themselves might spring to life. "Stay alert. If the traps back there were any indication, this won't be as simple as walking up and taking it."

"I'm aware," Aria replied, her eyes fixed on the fragment. The light emanating from it seemed alive, dancing in the dimness and casting rippling patterns across the walls. "I've never seen anything like this before."

"Neither have I," Torin admitted, though his voice held none of her wonder. "Which is why I'm waiting for it to try and kill us."

She shot him a look but didn't respond, her focus locked on the artifact. Slowly, she approached the pedestal, her steps cautious but deliberate. As she neared, the pulsing light intensified, as though the shard were reacting to her presence.

Torin's voice cut through the charged air. "Aria, don't just—"

"Wait," she interrupted, holding up a hand. "It's... calling to me."

Torin frowned, his hand resting on the hilt of his blade. "Calling to you? That doesn't sound like a good thing."

"It's not a voice," she explained, her brow furrowing. "It's more like a feeling. Like... it's waiting for me."

"That's exactly what worries me," Torin muttered, but he didn't stop her as she moved closer.

Aria reached the pedestal, her fingers trembling slightly as she extended her hand toward the shard. The air around it was warm, humming with energy that sent tingles racing up her arm. She hesitated for a moment, glancing back at Torin.

"This might hurt," she said, attempting a weak smile.

"Then don't touch it," he replied flatly.

"I don't think I have a choice," she said, turning back to the shard. Her hand hovered over it for a moment before she finally pressed her fingers against its smooth surface.

The world shifted.

A rush of images flooded her mind, sharp and vivid, each one crashing over her like a wave. She saw a sprawling landscape torn apart by rifts of glowing light, the ground cracking open as fire and shadow consumed the skies. Tribes of people, their faces painted in patterns she recognized from the villagers, clashed in brutal battles, their cries of anger and despair ringing in her ears.

"Stop!" Aria cried, but the visions didn't relent.

The scene changed. She stood on a battlefield, the world around her fractured and burning. A crown of light and shadow rested on her head, heavy and unyielding. Warriors knelt before her, their faces a mixture of hope and fear. Behind her, the jagged rifts pulsed with unstable energy, threatening to consume everything.

"You are the Shattered Queen," a voice echoed, deep and resonant, though it came from within her own mind. "You hold the balance. To unite or to destroy."

"No," Aria whispered, shaking her head as the crown's weight pressed harder. "This isn't me. I'm not—"

The vision shifted again. The tribes fought not each other but the rifts themselves, their spears and magic striking at the destructive forces tearing their world apart. Aria stood at the center of it all, her hands raised as streams of light poured from her, knitting the rifts together. But with every rift she sealed, more appeared, each one larger and more ferocious than the last.

The weight of it all crushed her. The crown, the power, the responsibility—it was too much. She gasped for air, her chest heaving as the images finally began to fade.

"Aria!" Torin's voice snapped her back to reality.

She stumbled back from the pedestal, the shard's glow dimming slightly as her hand fell away. Torin caught her before she could collapse, his strong grip steadying her as she clutched at his arm.

"Are you all right?" he asked, his tone urgent but laced with worry.

"I..." Her voice trembled, her hands still shaking as she tried to catch her breath. "I saw... everything. The rifts, the tribes, the fighting. It was chaos. And I was..." She swallowed hard, her throat dry. "I was in the middle of it. Leading them. Holding it all together."

Torin's eyes narrowed. "The prophecy."

"No," she said quickly, though her voice lacked conviction. "It's just the shard. It—it showed me something, but that doesn't mean it's real."

"You felt it, didn't you?" Torin pressed, his tone softening. "That power, that connection. You can deny it all you want, but you know it's real."

Aria shook her head, stepping away from him. "I don't want it to be real."

"Wanting doesn't matter," he said, his voice firm. "What matters is that you're tied to this. Whether it's the shard, the essence, or the prophecy, it's part of you now."

She turned back to the pedestal, her gaze fixed on the shard. Its light had returned to its steady pulse, as though nothing had happened. But Aria knew better. Something had changed—inside her, around her. She could feel it in the air, in the weight pressing against her chest.

"Let's just take it and go," she said finally, her voice hollow. "We'll figure it out later."

Torin nodded, but his expression remained tense. "Later might not be far off."

As they carefully removed the shard and turned to leave, Aria couldn't shake the lingering images from her mind. The fractured world, the warring tribes, and the crown of light and shadow—it all felt like a warning. Or worse, a promise.

Aria's legs gave way as she stumbled back from the pedestal, her breath ragged and uneven. The shard's glow dimmed behind her, the air around it no longer pulsing with the same intensity, but the weight of what she had seen clung to her like a shroud. Her chest heaved as she fought to steady herself, the vivid images of chaos and destruction still burning in her mind.

"Easy," Torin said, catching her by the arm before she could collapse completely. His grip was firm, steadying her as her knees buckled. "Take a breath."

"I can't," she gasped, her voice trembling. "Torin, I—what I saw—it was too much."

He crouched slightly, leveling his gaze with hers. "You're still here," he said quietly, though there was a hard edge to his tone. "You survived it. Now pull yourself together."

Her hands clutched at his arm as she tried to focus, the cold sweat on her brow making her shiver. "It wasn't just a vision," she said, her voice cracking. "It felt real. Like I was there. The tribes were fighting, the rifts were tearing everything apart, and I—" She broke off, shaking her head. "I can't be part of this, Torin. I can't."

Torin's jaw tightened, his dark eyes studying her intently. "You are part of it. Whether you want to be or not."

"No," she whispered, shaking her head vehemently. "I'm not the Shattered Queen. I'm not Seluna's chosen. I'm just—"

"Stop," Torin said sharply, cutting her off. His voice was calm, but his expression was grim. "You don't get to pretend this isn't happening. Not after what just happened back there. That shard reacted to you, Aria. It didn't choose me. It didn't choose anyone else. It chose you."

She stared at him, her breath catching as the truth of his words sank in. "But why me? I don't understand. I didn't ask for this."

"Do you think anyone does?" Torin replied, his voice hardening. "You think the villagers wanted to wait their whole lives for a prophecy to save them from falling apart? Or that I wanted to be tied to this mess, guarding someone I don't even know will survive it? None of us asked for this, Aria. But here we are."

Her grip on his arm tightened, her voice rising in frustration. "But I don't even know what I'm supposed to do! I'm not a warrior, or a leader, or whatever they think I'm supposed to be. I don't have magic—I don't even know how to control the little I do have!"

Torin sighed, his shoulders tensing as he looked away for a moment. When he turned back, his tone was quieter, but no less firm. "You don't have to understand it all right now. But you need to stop running from it. Denying it won't make it go away."

Aria felt tears prick at the corners of her eyes, her voice dropping to a whisper. "What if I fail? What if I can't do what they need me to do?"

Torin's expression softened slightly, though the weight of his words didn't. "Then the rifts will tear this world apart. The tribes will keep fighting until there's nothing left to save. That's what's at stake, Aria. This isn't just about you. It's bigger than all of us."

She looked down, her fingers trembling as she clenched them into fists. "It's too much," she said softly. "I don't know how to carry all of this."

"You don't carry it alone," Torin said, his voice steady. "You have people who will help you. The elders, the villagers... me. But you have to start accepting it. Otherwise, none of us have a chance."

She met his gaze, searching his eyes for reassurance. "Do you really believe I can do this?"

He hesitated, his expression unreadable for a moment. Then he gave a small nod. "I believe you don't have a choice. And I've seen what happens when people step up because they have to—not because they want to."

Her lips parted as if to argue, but she stopped herself, the weight of his words settling over her. She wiped at her face, taking a shaky breath. "Okay," she said finally, her voice barely audible. "Okay. But I don't know where to start."

Torin's mouth twitched in the faintest hint of a smirk. "You start by surviving. Everything else comes after that."

She managed a weak laugh, though it sounded more like a sob. "Great. Survive first, save the world later."

"Something like that," he said, his tone lightening just slightly. He straightened, offering her a hand. "Come on. We've got what we came for. Let's get out of here before this place decides to throw another trap at us."

Aria hesitated, then took his hand, letting him pull her to her feet. Her legs were still shaky, but she stood taller this time, her shoulders squaring slightly as she looked back at the pedestal. The shard's glow was faint now, almost subdued, but she could still feel its presence, like an ember burning deep within her.

As they turned to leave, Torin spoke again, his voice low. "Whatever happens next, Aria, remember this: the prophecy doesn't care what you believe. It cares what you do."

She didn't respond, but his words stayed with her as they made their way out of the ruins, the weight of the shard in her pack a constant reminder of the burden she now carried—and the uncertain road ahead.

Chapter 9
The First Fragment

The Obsidian Peaks rose like jagged teeth against the gray sky, their black stone glinting faintly in the weak sunlight. Aria and Torin approached the base of the mountains, their footsteps crunching on the loose gravel that marked the transition from the Crystal Sands to this foreboding terrain. The air was colder here, thin and sharp, carrying a strange electric charge that made the hair on the back of Aria's neck stand on end.

"Charming place," Aria muttered, pulling her cloak tighter around her shoulders. Her voice was thin, her attempt at levity failing to mask the growing unease in her chest.

"Keep your focus," Torin said, his tone as steady as ever. He walked a few paces ahead, his eyes scanning the jagged path that wound up toward the peaks. "The Shamans aren't known for their hospitality."

Aria huffed, stumbling slightly as her foot caught on a loose stone. "Fantastic. Another group of people who probably hate me on sight."

"It's not hate," Torin said, glancing back at her. "It's mistrust. They don't welcome outsiders easily, and the Shamans… they see more than most."

"That's comforting," Aria said dryly, adjusting her pack. "Anything else I should know before we meet them? Maybe some ritual dance or secret handshake?"

Torin's lips twitched, almost forming a smile. "Just be honest. They'll see through anything else."

"Honest," she repeated, rolling her eyes. "Sure. That always goes well."

The path grew steeper as they climbed, the peaks looming closer with every step. The air was heavy now, charged with an energy that made Aria's skin prickle. The jagged rocks seemed to pulse faintly, as though the mountains themselves were alive, watching.

By the time they reached the entrance to the Shamans' enclave, Aria's legs were burning, and her nerves were frayed. The opening was marked by a massive stone archway carved directly into the mountainside, its surface etched with runes that glowed faintly in the dim light.

Torin stopped, his posture rigid as he turned to face her. "This is it," he said. "Are you ready?"

"Do I have a choice?" she asked, her voice quieter now.

"No," he said simply, but his gaze softened. "Just remember—you don't face this alone."

Aria nodded, taking a deep breath. "Let's do this."

Together, they stepped through the archway, the air growing colder as they entered the dark passage beyond. The narrow tunnel twisted and turned, the faint glow of the runes their only source of light. The energy in the air grew stronger, pressing down on Aria's chest like an invisible weight.

Finally, the passage opened into a vast cavern. The ceiling was impossibly high, vanishing into shadows, while the floor was a smooth expanse of obsidian that reflected the faint light of torches mounted on the walls. Figures stood in a semi-circle at the center of the space, their cloaks as black as the stone beneath their feet. Their faces were hidden, their hoods pulled low, but Aria could feel their eyes on her, piercing and unrelenting.

Torin stepped forward, his movements careful but confident. "We come seeking the guidance of the Obsidian Shamans," he said, his voice carrying through the cavern.

One of the figures stepped forward, their movements slow and deliberate. When they spoke, their voice was low and resonant, echoing in the vast space. "The air carries your intent, but the Peaks do not welcome the unworthy. Why have you come?"

Aria swallowed hard, her mouth dry. She stepped forward, her hands clenched at her sides. "I'm here to end Morvan's curse," she said, her voice steadier than she expected. "The prophecy brought me here."

The Shaman tilted their head slightly, the faint glow of the torches reflecting off the edges of their hood. "The prophecy is a song sung by many voices, each with their own melody. What makes you believe you are the one destined to silence the discord?"

"I don't know if I'm destined," Aria admitted, her voice soft but resolute. "But I'm here. And I'm trying. That has to count for something."

There was a murmur among the other Shamans, their whispers blending with the faint hum of energy that filled the cavern. The lead Shaman raised a hand, silencing them.

"You carry the essence," they said, stepping closer. "It is faint, but it stirs within you. Perhaps you are what you claim to be. But the Peaks will judge."

"What does that mean?" Aria asked, her anxiety spiking.

"The Peaks demand truth," the Shaman said. "They will strip away the lies you tell yourself and reveal the path you must walk. If you are not ready, they will destroy you."

Aria's breath hitched, her heart pounding. "Sounds… fun."

"It is not meant to be," the Shaman replied. "Prepare yourself."

Torin stepped beside her, his voice low. "You can do this."

She looked up at him, his calm presence grounding her. "You really believe that?"

"Yes," he said, his tone firm. "Because I've seen what you can do. And because you've made it this far."

Aria nodded, taking another deep breath. The Peaks buzzed with energy, and the Shamans' gaze felt like a weight pressing down on her. But despite the fear coiling in her chest, she felt a flicker of resolve.

"Let's get this over with," she said, her voice steady.

The Shamans parted, their movements as fluid as shadows, revealing a narrow path that led deeper into the mountains. The lead Shaman gestured toward it. "The Rite of Shadows awaits. Step forward, if you dare."

Aria glanced at Torin one last time. His eyes met hers, unwavering.

"You've got this," he said quietly.

She squared her shoulders and stepped onto the path, the hum of the Peaks growing louder with every step.

The air grew colder as Aria stepped deeper into the mountain. The narrow path opened into a vast cavern, its walls glinting faintly in the low light of a pale, otherworldly glow. She hesitated at the threshold, the weight of the place pressing on her chest. It wasn't just the stillness or the chill that unnerved her—it was the feeling that the cavern itself was alive, watching.

Torin's steadying presence was gone. The Shamans had insisted she enter alone, warning that the Hall of Echoes would strip away all pretense. Whatever awaited her within, she would face it on her own.

Aria inhaled deeply, steadying herself. "You've come this far," she whispered, her voice small against the vastness of the space. "You can do this."

Her boots echoed softly on the obsidian floor as she stepped forward. The air grew thicker, charged with a strange, buzzing energy. She glanced around, her eyes adjusting to the dim light. The walls were lined with jagged crystals, each one glowing faintly, pulsing in time with her heartbeat.

Then, the whispers began.

At first, they were faint, barely audible over the sound of her own breath. But as she moved deeper into the cavern, they grew louder, overlapping in a chaotic symphony of voices. They came from every direction, surrounding her, filling her mind with fragmented words and phrases.

"Sacrifice… unity… the bridge must hold…"

"Who's there?" Aria called, her voice trembling. The whispers didn't answer, but they swirled around her, relentless and unyielding. She pressed her hands to her ears, but it did nothing to block the sound. It wasn't just in the air—it was in her head.

She stumbled forward, the pulsing crystals casting flickering shadows that seemed to shift and move on their own. Her chest tightened, her breathing shallow as the whispers grew louder.

Then, suddenly, the voices stopped.

The silence was deafening, pressing down on her like a physical weight. Aria straightened, glancing around the cavern. The stillness was unnerving, the absence of sound making her ears ring.

"You've come far."

The voice was soft, melodic, and familiar. Aria turned sharply, her eyes widening as a figure emerged from the shadows. It was Maelis, her form bathed in a faint, golden light. She looked just as Aria had seen her in the visions—regal and commanding, yet haunted by something deep and sorrowful.

"Maelis," Aria breathed, her voice barely a whisper.

Maelis inclined her head, her violet eyes locking onto Aria's. "You carry the essence, but you doubt its purpose."

"I don't doubt it," Aria said quickly. "I just... I don't understand it."

"That is not the same," Maelis replied, her tone gentle but firm. She stepped closer, her movements fluid and ethereal. "The essence is not a weapon to wield or a burden to carry. It is a thread, binding all things together. Without unity, it is nothing."

"Unity?" Aria repeated, frowning. "You mean the clans? The prophecy?"

Maelis didn't answer directly. Instead, she raised a hand, and the cavern around them shifted. The crystals flared brightly, casting the walls into sharp relief. Shadows danced and twisted, forming images—armies clashing, rivers of essence flowing, and a figure standing alone at the center of it all.

"You are the bridge," Maelis said, her voice low but resonant. "Between the light and the shadow, the broken and the whole. But a bridge must be strong, or it will collapse."

Aria swallowed hard, her throat tight. "What if I'm not strong enough?"

Maelis stepped closer, her gaze piercing. "Strength is not the absence of fear. It is the will to stand despite it."

The images around them shifted again, showing Maelis herself standing at the edge of a great chasm, her hands glowing with elemental power. The shadowy figures swarmed toward her, an endless tide of darkness, but she held her ground, her expression fierce.

"You stood alone," Aria said softly. "You fought until the end. I don't think I can do that."

Maelis reached out, her hand brushing against Aria's shoulder. The touch was warm, grounding. "You are not me," she said. "But you are not alone."

The shadows faded, and the cavern returned to its original form, the crystals dimming once more. Maelis's light began to waver, her form becoming less distinct.

"Wait," Aria said, panic rising in her chest. "What am I supposed to do? How do I fix this?"

"Unity," Maelis whispered, her voice fading like a distant echo. "And sacrifice."

The golden light flickered and vanished, leaving Aria standing alone in the cavern. The silence returned, heavier than before, and she realized she was trembling. Her mind raced, trying to piece together Maelis's cryptic words.

"Unity and sacrifice," she repeated aloud, her voice hollow. "What does that even mean?"

The crystals pulsed faintly, as if in response, but the cavern remained still. With a deep breath, Aria turned and began walking back toward the entrance. The Shamans' challenge had shaken her, but it had also left her with something she hadn't expected—a faint, fragile hope.

Maelis's words echoed in her mind as she stepped back into the cold mountain air. She didn't know what lay ahead, but for the first time, she felt a glimmer of clarity. The path was still unclear, but she would walk it, step by step, until she found the answers she needed.

The Hall of Echoes had transformed. Where before there was an eerie stillness, the space now pulsed with an oppressive energy. The crystals embedded in the walls glowed faintly, casting long, distorted shadows that twisted unnaturally. At the center of the cavern, a swirling vortex of shadow essence coiled like a living thing, its dark tendrils reaching hungrily for the edges of the room.

Aria stood at the edge of the vortex, her breaths shallow and rapid. The Obsidian Shamans encircled her, their cloaks blending seamlessly into the darkness. Their leader stepped forward, their hood obscuring their face, but the power radiating from them was undeniable.

"The Rite of Shadows is not for the weak of will," the leader intoned, their voice reverberating through the cavern. "It will test the very core of who you are. Fail, and the shadows will consume you."

Aria swallowed hard, her hands clenched at her sides. "And if I succeed?"

"Then you will wield the essence of shadow," the leader replied. "You will prove yourself worthy of our loyalty."

Torin's voice broke through the tension. "She's ready," he said firmly, stepping to Aria's side. His presence was steady, grounding. "You've seen what she's capable of."

The Shaman turned their hooded head toward him. "The shadows do not care for words, warrior. They care only for strength."

"I've made it this far," Aria said, her voice steady despite the fear curling in her chest. "What do I have to do?"

The Shaman gestured to the vortex. "Enter the shadows. They will test you. Only when you master them will you emerge."

Aria took a deep breath, her gaze flicking to Torin. His expression was unreadable, but there was a faint edge of concern in his eyes.

"You've got this," he said quietly. "Remember, the shadows only show what's already inside you. Don't let them control you."

Easier said than done, she thought but didn't say it aloud. Instead, she gave him a small nod and stepped toward the vortex.

The moment she crossed the threshold, the world shifted.

The shadows swallowed her whole, and Aria found herself standing in complete darkness. It wasn't the absence of light; it was something more tangible, more alive. The air felt heavy, pressing against her skin, and the faint sound of whispers filled her ears.

"You are weak."

The voice was hers, but distorted, twisted into something cruel. Aria turned, searching for the source, but the darkness stretched endlessly in every direction.

"You don't belong here."

She clenched her fists, her breath quickening. "This is just a trick," she said aloud, her voice trembling. "You're not real."

A figure emerged from the shadows, stepping toward her. It was her, but not. This version of herself was stronger, more confident, but her eyes burned with a cold, unfeeling light.

"Are you so sure?" the shadow version said, a smirk curling on her lips. "You've stumbled through this world, clinging to hope and luck. What makes you think you can succeed?"

"I've made it this far," Aria said, though her voice wavered.

The shadow laughed, the sound cutting through the darkness like a blade. "By chance, not by strength. You're nothing but a pretender, a weakling pretending to be a savior."

Aria's chest tightened, the words hitting harder than she wanted to admit. "No," she said, louder this time. "I'm trying. That has to count for something."

"Trying won't save you," the shadow sneered. "Trying won't save them."

The darkness around her shifted, forming shapes—Torin, the Verdant Clans, the Dune Wanderers. Each figure twisted and fell, consumed by the shadows, their screams piercing the air. Aria's heart pounded as she reached for them, but they dissolved before her eyes.

"No!" she shouted. "That's not real!"

The shadow version of herself stepped closer, her expression hard. "It could be. If you fail."

Aria closed her eyes, her fists shaking at her sides. The fear was overwhelming, clawing at her mind, but beneath it was something else—a spark of defiance.

"You're right," she said softly, opening her eyes. "I could fail. But I won't stop trying."

The shadow tilted its head, its smirk fading.

Aria stepped forward, her voice growing stronger. "I'm scared. I don't know if I'm strong enough. But I'm still here. And that's more than you can say."

The shadow hissed, its form flickering. Aria reached out, her hand cutting through the darkness. The shadow dissolved, and the whispers faded, replaced by a steady hum. The oppressive weight lifted, and the swirling shadows around her stilled, coalescing into a faint, glowing orb of dark light.

She reached out and grasped the orb. It was cool to the touch, and as she held it, a surge of power coursed through her veins. The shadows no longer felt like enemies—they were part of her now, a tool she could wield.

The darkness dissolved, and Aria stumbled back into the cavern. The Shamans watched in silence as she caught her breath, the glowing orb still cradled in her hand.

"She has passed," the leader said, their voice filled with something close to reverence. "The shadows have accepted her."

Torin was at her side in an instant, steadying her with a hand on her shoulder. "You did it," he said, his voice low.

Aria nodded, her breaths still ragged. "I think… I understand now. The shadows weren't trying to break me. They were trying to show me who I am."

The Shaman stepped forward, bowing their head slightly. "You have proven yourself, Aria. The Obsidian Shamans will stand with you."

For the first time, Aria felt the weight of the shadows lessen, replaced by a quiet sense of strength. She had faced herself, her fears, and her doubts—and she had emerged whole.

The cavern felt quieter now, the oppressive weight of the shadows lifted as if the mountain itself had exhaled. Aria stood in the center of the Hall, the faint glow of the shadow orb still pulsing faintly in her hands. Her body ached with exhaustion, and her breaths came in shallow bursts, but beneath the fatigue was something stronger—a sense of triumph.

Torin stepped toward her, his movements uncharacteristically slow, as though he didn't want to disturb the fragile moment. His dark eyes locked onto hers, and for the first time, there was no trace of his usual guardedness. Instead, his expression was open, filled with something that made her chest tighten.

"You did it," he said quietly, his voice low but steady.

Aria managed a weak smile, her fingers tightening around the orb. "Barely. I thought those shadows were going to tear me apart."

"They tried," he said, his tone softening. "But they couldn't. You didn't let them."

She looked down at the orb, its light dimming as the essence settled within her. "It wasn't just me," she said, her voice thoughtful. "They showed me my worst fears, my doubts. But… I don't know. I felt like I wasn't alone. Like everything I've been through brought me here, and somehow, that was enough."

Torin nodded, stepping closer until he was standing directly in front of her. His gaze lingered on her face, and for a moment, the only sound in the cavern was the faint hum of the crystals.

"You're stronger than you think, Aria," he said finally. "You've faced more in these last few weeks than most people face in a lifetime. And you're still standing."

"Barely," she repeated, her laugh soft but genuine this time.

"Standing is standing," Torin said, a faint smile tugging at the corners of his lips. "You've earned this."

Aria searched his face, trying to find the usual sharp edges of his demeanor, but they weren't there. Instead, there was a warmth that made her pulse quicken. "I didn't think you believed in me," she said, her voice quieter now.

"I've always believed in you," Torin replied, his tone earnest. "Maybe I didn't say it enough, but I did. I do."

Her throat tightened, and she glanced away, overwhelmed by the weight of his words. "Thanks," she said softly. "That means... more than you know."

Torin reached out, his hand brushing against hers as he gestured to the orb. "And now you have this. The Shamans won't just follow anyone. You've proven yourself to them—and to me."

Aria's gaze flicked back to his, her heart pounding in her chest. There was something unspoken in his expression, a promise that felt both daunting and comforting. "What happens now?" she asked, her voice barely above a whisper.

"We keep going," he said, his voice steady. "But we do it together. Whatever comes next, we face it as a team."

Aria nodded, her grip on the orb tightening. "Together," she echoed, the word feeling heavier than it should.

The Shamans, who had been silently observing, stepped forward. Their leader inclined their head toward Aria, their voice reverent. "You have passed the Rite of Shadows, Aria. The essence has chosen you, and so do we."

Aria blinked, momentarily caught off guard. "You mean... you'll help us?"

"We will follow," the leader said simply. "The Obsidian Peaks stand with you."

She turned to Torin, her expression a mixture of relief and disbelief. "Did that really just happen?"

He smirked, his usual edge returning. "It did. And I told you it would."

She rolled her eyes but couldn't stop the smile spreading across her face. "I guess you did."

Torin's smirk softened, and he reached out, clasping her shoulder. "You've earned their loyalty, Aria. And mine."

Her breath caught at the weight of his words. For a moment, the prophecy, the trials, even the looming threat of Morvan seemed distant. All that mattered was the warmth in Torin's eyes and the unspoken promise between them.

"Let's not make it a habit," she said, her tone teasing despite the emotion in her voice. "I can't handle too many heartfelt moments in one day."

Torin chuckled, his hand falling back to his side. "Don't get used to it."

They shared a look, the silence between them carrying more meaning than words could capture. Then, with a deep breath, Aria straightened, the orb in her hand glowing faintly as if in response to her renewed determination.

"Ready?" Torin asked.

"Always," she replied, and together, they turned to face the path ahead.

Chapter 10
Bonds Forged in Strife

The village hummed with quiet activity as the sun dipped low on the horizon, painting the sky in hues of orange and purple. Smoke from small fires curled into the air, carrying the earthy scent of herbs and roasting meat. Aria sat cross-legged in the center of a circle, surrounded by villagers who murmured softly in their melodic language. Before her, an elder traced shapes into the dirt with a slender stick, her gestures slow and deliberate.

Aria furrowed her brow, trying to make sense of the symbols being drawn. They seemed familiar in a way she couldn't place—like pieces of a puzzle she was meant to solve but couldn't quite fit together. "I don't understand," she said, her voice tinged with frustration.

The elder looked up, her silver hair gleaming in the fading light. She spoke gently, her words flowing like a song, but the language barrier rendered them meaningless to Aria. The other villagers nodded solemnly, their eyes fixed on her with expressions of expectation.

"She's explaining the prophecy," Torin said, standing nearby with his arms crossed. He leaned against a wooden post, watching the exchange with a mix of amusement and exasperation. "Or, at least, she's trying to."

Aria shot him a look. "That's helpful. Why don't you translate, then?"

"I would if I could," Torin replied, shrugging. "Their dialect isn't the same as the one I know. Besides, they're big on metaphor. Even if I did understand, it probably wouldn't make sense."

"Great," Aria muttered, turning her attention back to the elder. "So I'm supposed to piece this all together without knowing what anyone's actually saying?"

The elder gestured to the symbols she had drawn: a jagged line splitting a circle, a series of radiating waves, and a figure standing with arms outstretched. Her voice rose slightly, her tone insistent, as if willing Aria to grasp their meaning.

"She's talking about balance," Torin said, his gaze narrowing as he studied the symbols. "The rifts—see how the circle is fractured? That's the world breaking apart. The figure is supposed to be you."

Aria frowned, her fingers brushing the dirt. "Why is it always me? Why can't it be anyone else?"

Torin's smirk was fleeting, but his tone was serious. "Because you're the one the shard chose. And because the elders believe you're Seluna's chosen. Whether you like it or not."

Aria sighed heavily, pushing herself to her feet. "I don't even know what 'balance' is supposed to mean. How am I supposed to fix something I don't understand?"

One of the younger villagers, a girl no older than thirteen, approached hesitantly, holding out a small bundle of leaves tied with twine. Her wide, dark eyes were filled with both awe and fear. She spoke a single word—"Seluna"—and held the bundle higher.

Aria blinked, unsure how to respond. "Uh... thank you?" she said awkwardly, reaching for the bundle. The girl bowed her head and quickly scurried back to the others.

Torin chuckled softly. "You're practically royalty now."

"Don't remind me," Aria muttered, unwrapping the bundle. Inside were a handful of dried herbs and a small carved charm shaped like a crescent moon. "What is this?"

"Essence protection," Torin explained. "The herbs are supposed to help ward off corruption from the rifts. The charm is symbolic—Seluna's light, guiding you in the darkness."

Aria stared at the items, her expression conflicted. "They really believe this, don't they?"

"They don't just believe it," Torin said, his tone softer now. "It's their reality. The rifts are real, the danger is real, and so is their faith in you. Whether or not you think you're the Shattered Queen, they need you to be."

Before Aria could respond, the elder spoke again, gesturing for her to follow. The other villagers murmured and began to move, gathering supplies and preparing for the next leg of the journey. Aria hesitated, glancing at Torin.

"She wants to show you something," he said. "Go. I'll make sure the rest is ready."

Reluctantly, Aria followed the elder, who led her to a small hut near the edge of the village. Inside, the walls were lined with woven mats and shelves holding bowls of essence-infused water and bundles of herbs. At the center of the room was a simple wooden pedestal, upon which rested an intricately carved stone tablet. Its surface was etched with more symbols—similar to those drawn in the dirt but far more detailed.

The elder gestured for Aria to kneel and pointed to the tablet. Her voice rose in a rhythmic chant, the cadence both calming and unsettling. Aria leaned closer, tracing the carvings with her fingers.

"What does it say?" she whispered, her voice tinged with curiosity and dread.

Torin's voice came from the doorway. "It's part of the prophecy. They've been preserving it here for generations."

Aria turned to him, her eyes wide. "Can you read it?"

"Not all of it," he admitted, stepping into the hut. "But I recognize some of the symbols. That one—" he pointed to a spiral near the top, "represents the rifts. And here—" he traced a jagged line cutting through the spiral, "this is the balance the Shattered Queen is supposed to restore."

"And this one?" Aria asked, pointing to a crescent-shaped mark near the bottom.

Torin hesitated. "That... I don't know. It could mean light, or guidance, or even destruction, depending on the context."

"Helpful," Aria muttered, her frustration mounting. "So I'm supposed to take these cryptic symbols, some dried leaves, and blind faith, and save the world?"

Torin smirked faintly. "Sounds about right."

She glared at him but couldn't hold back a faint laugh. "This is impossible."

"Maybe," Torin said, his tone softening. "But you're not alone. Remember that."

Aria looked back at the tablet, the weight of its meaning pressing heavily on her. She didn't understand it yet, but she couldn't shake the feeling that whatever came next would demand more of her than she was ready to give.

The jungle was alive with its usual symphony of chirping insects and distant bird calls, but the sound was less oppressive now, blending into the rhythm of their footsteps. The heat pressed down on them, and though the path ahead was as tangled and overgrown as ever, Aria felt a strange calm settle over her. They had left the village at dawn, the morning light casting long shadows through the dense canopy above.

Torin walked a few steps ahead, his movements efficient and confident. His blade rested on his hip, his hand never straying far from it, as if he were always ready for an attack.

"You're always so tense," Aria said after a long silence, quickening her pace to walk beside him. "Do you ever relax?"

He glanced at her briefly, his expression unreadable. "Not when I'm out here."

"Do you ever relax anywhere?" she pressed, a faint smirk tugging at her lips.

Torin didn't answer immediately. His eyes scanned the path ahead, his jaw tightening. "I'll relax when the rifts stop tearing this world apart."

Aria sighed, kicking at a loose root as they walked. "You're impossible, you know that? Everything with you is life or death."

"Because it is," he replied flatly. "This isn't a game, Aria. It's survival."

"Sure, but you don't have to be such a brooding hero about it," she said, her tone light. "I mean, we're not fighting a shadow panther right now. It's okay to be human."

His lips twitched, almost forming a smile. "Is this your way of telling me to lighten up?"

"It's my way of telling you that you're allowed to have a personality beyond 'grumpy warrior,'" she teased.

Torin exhaled sharply, a sound somewhere between a laugh and a scoff. "You don't know what you're asking for."

Aria tilted her head, intrigued. "Maybe not, but now I'm curious. You've been stuck with me for weeks, and I still don't know much about you. Where did you grow up?"

He hesitated, his gaze flickering to her before returning to the path. "A village. Small. It's gone now."

"Gone?" she echoed, her brow furrowing. "What happened?"

Torin's jaw tightened, and for a moment, she thought he wouldn't answer. But then he spoke, his voice quieter than usual. "The rifts happened. My village was on the borderlands. We didn't even know what was coming until it was too late."

Aria's teasing smile faded. "I'm sorry. I didn't know."

"Why would you?" he replied, shrugging. "It was years ago. Most of the borderland villages were wiped out. Those of us who survived... we learned to fight. To protect what little was left."

"That's how you became a warrior," she guessed, her voice softer now.

Torin nodded. "It wasn't a choice. It was survival. People like me—we don't get the luxury of choosing our paths."

"That's not fair," Aria said, her tone tinged with frustration. "You shouldn't have had to bear that kind of burden."

"Fairness doesn't exist in a world that's breaking apart," he said bluntly. "You learn that quickly on the borderlands."

They walked in silence for a few moments, the weight of his words settling over them. Aria glanced at him, her curiosity undimmed despite the tension in his voice.

"You're carrying a lot, aren't you?" she asked carefully. "Not just the fighting, but... something more."

Torin's eyes narrowed slightly, but he didn't stop walking. "What are you trying to get at?"

"I don't know," she admitted. "You just seem... heavier, somehow. Like there's something else you're not saying."

His expression hardened. "Some things are better left unsaid."

"Maybe," she said, refusing to back down. "But sometimes talking helps."

Torin stopped abruptly, turning to face her. His eyes were darker than usual, shadowed by something she couldn't quite name. "You want to know why I fight? Why I care so much about this prophecy?"

"Yes," she said, meeting his gaze. "I do."

He hesitated, his hands clenching into fists at his sides. "Because if it's real—if the prophecy is true—it might be the only chance we have to fix what's been broken. To stop more villages from being destroyed. To stop more people from losing everything."

Aria blinked, taken aback by the rawness in his voice. "You really believe that, don't you?"

"I have to," he said simply. "Because if I don't, then everything I've fought for, everything I've lost... it's all meaningless."

She looked at him, her chest tightening at the weight of his words. "Torin... I didn't realize."

He shook his head, his expression softening slightly. "You couldn't have. And it doesn't matter. What matters is that we keep going. That we find a way to make this prophecy work."

Aria nodded slowly, her voice quieter now. "You carry all of this, and yet you still help me. Why?"

His lips twitched again, almost forming a smile. "Because whether or not you believe in the prophecy, the shard chose you. And because... I believe you're stronger than you think you are."

Her breath caught at his words, and for a moment, she didn't know how to respond. The walls he kept so carefully built around himself had cracked, just enough for her to see the man behind them. And in that moment, she realized that maybe they weren't so different after all.

"Thank you," she said finally, her voice steady.

Torin nodded, turning back to the path. "Don't thank me yet. The hard part hasn't even started."

She smiled faintly, her steps lighter now as she followed him into the dense jungle.

The air grew colder as the jungle thinned, the dense canopy giving way to patches of open terrain. A low hum filled the air, faint at first but steadily growing louder, vibrating through the ground beneath Aria's boots. She paused, glancing uneasily at Torin.

"Do you feel that?" she asked, her voice barely audible.

Torin nodded, his expression grim. "It's the essence. It's unstable here."

Aria frowned, taking a cautious step forward. "Unstable? What does that mean exactly?"

"It means we're too close to a rift," Torin said, his hand tightening on the hilt of his blade. "The energy leaks into the surrounding land, twisting it. Be ready for anything."

Aria's stomach churned as she followed his gaze. Up ahead, the earth was fractured, deep fissures cutting through the terrain. A faint glow emanated from within the cracks, a sickly blue-green light that pulsed in irregular bursts. The air smelled sharp and metallic, making her nose sting.

"This... isn't normal," she said, her voice trembling. "How far does it go?"

Torin's jaw tightened as he surveyed the area. "Hard to say. The rifts spread faster when the essence is unstable. And without unity among the tribes, there's no one to contain it."

She turned to him, her brows furrowed. "Contain it how? How do you stop something like this?"

"The tribes used to have ways," Torin replied, his tone clipped. "Rituals, essence-bound artifacts, warriors trained to seal the rifts. But that was before they turned against each other."

"And now?"

"Now, they barely speak to one another, let alone work together," Torin said, his voice bitter. "They're too busy fighting over who's to blame for the rifts instead of stopping them."

Aria stared at the fractures in the ground, her chest tightening. "So what happens if they don't stop?"

Torin gave her a hard look. "The rifts grow. The fractures spread. Entire villages disappear. And eventually, the whole of Ilyria tears itself apart."

The weight of his words settled over her like a stone. "That's... a lot of pressure," she said softly, glancing back at the glowing fissures. "And they expect me to fix this."

"They don't just expect it," Torin said, his voice sharp but not unkind. "They need you to. Whether you believe in the prophecy or not, you're the only one with the shard. The only one the essence responds to."

"I don't even know where to start," she admitted, her voice breaking. "Look at this place, Torin. It's already falling apart."

"Then start here," Torin said, gesturing to the fractured ground. "Understand what's happening. See it for what it is."

Aria hesitated, her gaze lingering on the fissures. The glow seemed to pulse in rhythm with her own heartbeat, as if the rift itself was alive. She crouched down, her fingers brushing the edge of one crack. A faint warmth radiated from it, tingling against her skin.

"It's... alive, isn't it?" she asked, her voice barely above a whisper.

"In a way," Torin said, kneeling beside her. "The essence isn't just energy. It's connected to everything—the land, the people, even the air we breathe. When it's stable, it sustains life. When it's unstable..." He gestured to the fractures. "This happens."

"And the tribes used to manage this?" she asked, glancing at him. "How?"

"Together," he said simply. "The rituals required unity, a balance of knowledge and power that no single tribe could achieve on their own. They trusted each other, relied on each other. But that trust is gone now."

"Because of the rifts?"

"No," Torin said, his expression darkening. "Because of greed. Fear. Old wounds that never healed. The rifts are just the consequence of their division."

Aria sighed, standing and brushing dirt from her hands. "So not only do I have to stop the rifts, but I also have to fix centuries of tribal infighting. Anything else I should know about?"

Torin smirked faintly, though his tone remained serious. "It's not impossible, Aria. But it starts with you accepting that this is your fight now."

Her eyes narrowed. "You make it sound so simple."

"It's not," he admitted. "But you're here for a reason. You've seen what the essence can do. You've felt it. That connection is your greatest strength—and your greatest responsibility."

She looked away, her gaze drifting to the fissures again. The glow was stronger now, brighter, as though it were reacting to their presence. The hum in the air grew louder, making the ground beneath her feet vibrate.

"Torin," she said cautiously, taking a step back. "Is it supposed to do that?"

His hand flew to his blade as he followed her gaze. "No. Move—now!"

Before she could react, a burst of energy shot up from one of the fissures, sending a wave of heat and light rippling through the air. Aria stumbled, shielding her face with her arms as the ground beneath her shook violently.

Torin grabbed her arm, pulling her back. "We need to get out of here. Now!"

"What about the rift?" she shouted over the roar of the energy surge.

"We can't seal it without the tribes' help!" Torin yelled, dragging her toward higher ground. "This is what happens when the essence is left unchecked."

As they climbed to safety, Aria looked back at the glowing fractures, her heart pounding. The rift wasn't just a problem—it was a warning. And for the first time, she truly understood the stakes.

The roar of the unstable rift had faded into the distance, replaced by the quiet hum of the jungle around them. Aria sat on a fallen log, her elbows on her knees and her head bowed. Sweat clung to her skin, and her chest still heaved from their frantic escape. Torin paced a few feet away, his blade sheathed but his hand still resting on the hilt, as though he expected trouble to leap out from the shadows at any moment.

For a while, neither of them spoke. The weight of the fractured ground and the glowing fissures lingered heavily in the air, pressing on Aria's thoughts like an invisible hand.

"I've never seen anything like that," she said finally, her voice quiet but steady. She looked up at Torin, her eyes tired but determined. "It's worse than I thought."

Torin stopped pacing, turning to face her. "That was just one rift. There are dozens—hundreds—like it. And they're all growing worse."

She ran a hand through her hair, exhaling deeply. "How did it get this bad? If the tribes used to handle this, why didn't anyone stop it before now?"

"Because they couldn't," Torin said, crossing his arms. "The tribes have been at odds for so long they barely function as a collective anymore. The elders argue over whose fault it is instead of doing anything to fix it. They don't trust each other enough to perform the rituals."

Aria frowned, her gaze drifting to the ground. "And now they're pinning all their hopes on me."

"Because you're the only one who's shown the essence can respond," Torin said firmly. "You're not just part of this, Aria—you're the key to it."

She looked up sharply. "I don't want to be the key, Torin. I didn't ask for this."

"No one asks for it," he replied, his tone softer now. "But it doesn't change what's happening. You've seen it yourself—the rifts are tearing Ilyria apart. If you don't help, no one else can."

Her fingers clenched around the edge of the log. "You don't understand. Back in the village, with the shard, I saw things. Whole tribes at war. The land fracturing. A crown of light and shadow—" She shook her head. "It felt like a warning. Like no matter what I do, it won't be enough."

Torin stepped closer, crouching in front of her so their eyes were level. "Ilyria isn't gone yet. It's still here, still fighting. And so are you."

"But what if I fail?" she whispered. "What if I can't fix this? What if the prophecy isn't real, or worse—what if I'm not who they think I am?"

He didn't answer right away, his dark eyes searching hers. Then, with a quiet sigh, he said, "If you fail, then at least you'll know you tried. That you didn't stand by and let the world fall apart. That's more than anyone else is doing."

His words struck something deep inside her. She looked away, her hands tightening into fists. "It's not about the prophecy for me," she said after a moment. "I still don't know if I believe in it. But I can't keep ignoring what's happening around me. The rifts, the tribes... people are dying, Torin."

He nodded slowly. "And you're in a position to do something about it."

She looked back at him, her expression resolute. "Then I will. I'll find the rest of the prophecy fragments, not because some shard glowed when I touched it or because the villagers are calling me Seluna's chosen. I'll do it because I can't stand by and watch this world fall apart."

A faint smile touched Torin's lips. "That's a start."

Aria stood, brushing off her hands. "You'll help me, right? I'm going to need someone who knows how to navigate this mess."

He rose as well, his hand dropping from his blade to his side. "You'll have my blade and my guidance, as long as you're committed."

"I am," she said firmly, her eyes bright with determination. "I don't know what the prophecy means, or even if it's real, but I can't let the rifts win. If finding the fragments will help stop them, then that's what I'll do."

Torin held her gaze for a moment, then nodded. "Good. Because this journey isn't going to get easier. The fragments are scattered across Ilyria, and the closer we get, the more dangerous it'll be."

"I wouldn't expect anything less," Aria said, a faint smile tugging at her lips despite the gravity of their situation.

Torin allowed himself a brief smirk. "Then let's move. The rifts won't wait, and neither will the tribes."

As they set off again, the jungle seemed quieter, the air heavier with the tension of what lay ahead. But for the first time, Aria felt a flicker of clarity amidst the chaos. She wasn't ready to embrace destiny, but she couldn't deny the responsibility growing heavier with each step.

And if that meant confronting the shards, the rifts, and her own doubts head-on, so be it. She wouldn't stand by while Ilyria fell. Not anymore.

Chapter 11
The Rift's Reach

The air grew heavier as Aria and Torin led the group deeper into the jagged terrain surrounding the Obsidian Nexus. The landscape was stark and alien, with sharp black stone jutting out of the earth like the teeth of some great beast. A faint hum vibrated through the air, the telltale sign of the Nexus's power growing stronger with every step.

Aria tightened her grip on the staff she'd acquired from the Shamans, its faintly glowing runes the only light in the gathering gloom. Behind her, the sound of shifting armor and murmured complaints from the clans filled the air. The tension was palpable, like a storm brewing just out of sight.

"We shouldn't be here," Khoran muttered, his voice low but carrying easily in the eerie quiet. "This place is cursed."

Kaela, walking a few steps ahead of him, shot him a glare over her shoulder. "Everything's cursed to you, Khoran. If you're so scared, maybe you should head back to the fire and leave the real work to us."

"Watch your tongue," Khoran snapped, his hand brushing the hilt of his blade. "I've fought for these clans longer than you've been alive."

"And yet you've done nothing but complain since we left camp," Kaela retorted, her voice sharp. "Maybe it's time you learned to listen instead of grumbling like an old man."

"Enough," Torin barked, his tone cutting through the argument. He didn't look back, his eyes fixed on the path ahead. "If you want to argue, do it when we're not on the edge of hostile territory."

The group fell silent, though Khoran's glare lingered. Aria glanced back at Torin, her voice quiet. "They're getting worse."

"They're scared," he replied without breaking stride. "And scared people are dangerous."

She nodded, her gaze drifting to the distant horizon. "Do you think they'll hold together when it counts?"

Torin's jaw tightened. "I don't know. But if they don't, it won't matter how strong we are."

Aria sighed, the weight of his words settling heavily on her. She slowed her pace slightly, letting the others move ahead, and fell into step beside Torin. "You don't have to carry all of this, you know," she said softly. "It's not just on you."

Torin gave her a sidelong glance, his expression softening. "Feels like it is, sometimes."

"It's not," she said firmly. "We're in this together. All of us."

He didn't respond immediately, his gaze focused on the jagged peaks rising in the distance. Finally, he said, "You're better at believing that than I am."

Aria opened her mouth to respond, but Kaela's voice cut through the quiet. "We're close," she called back, her tone laced with unease. "The energy's stronger here."

Torin nodded, his posture stiffening. "Stay sharp. The Nexus doesn't just radiate power—it attracts things."

Khoran scoffed, though his hand lingered on his weapon. "Things like what?"

"Things you don't want to meet," Torin said grimly. "And if we're unlucky, Morvan's forces."

The name hung in the air like a shadow, sending a ripple of unease through the group. Aria tightened her grip on her staff, her heart pounding. The Nexus was close, its power thrumming through her veins, but the tension between the clans was almost worse than the danger ahead.

As they rounded a jagged outcrop, the path opened up into a wide plateau. At its center, the Nexus pulsed with dark energy, a swirling vortex of shadow and light that seemed to draw the very air toward it. The hum in the air grew louder, vibrating through Aria's bones.

"Gods," Kaela muttered, her eyes wide. "I've never seen anything like it."

Khoran snorted, though there was a flicker of unease in his expression. "Looks like a death trap to me."

"It's a source of power," Aria said, stepping forward. "The Shamans said it's tied to the essence—and to Morvan. If we can reach it—"

"Reach it and do what?" Khoran interrupted, his voice sharp. "You think you can just walk into that thing and make everything better?"

"That's the plan," Torin said dryly, his tone edged with irritation. "Unless you have a better idea."

Khoran's mouth opened, then closed, his glare darkening. "This is madness."

"Madness is doing nothing while Morvan tears Ilyria apart," Aria shot back, her voice rising. "If you don't want to be here, Khoran, then leave. But stop holding us back."

The words hung in the air, the group watching the exchange with a mix of unease and curiosity. Khoran's face twisted with anger, but he said nothing, stepping back into the crowd.

Torin's voice broke the tension. "We move together. No one splits off, and no one takes unnecessary risks. Keep your weapons ready and your wits sharper."

Aria nodded, her resolve hardening as she turned her gaze back to the Nexus. The path ahead was fraught with danger, but there was no turning back. They would face whatever lay ahead together—or not at all.

The air around the Nexus grew colder, a biting chill that seeped into Aria's bones. The hum of the swirling shadow energy had shifted, its rhythm more erratic, like a heartbeat speeding up in fear or anticipation. As she approached the edge of the vortex, a sudden wave of dizziness struck her, forcing her to stumble back.

"Aria!" Torin's voice cut through the haze, sharp with concern. His hand gripped her arm, steadying her. "What's wrong?"

"I—I don't know," she murmured, pressing a hand to her temple. The world around her wavered, the jagged rocks and swirling shadows blurring into a distorted mess. "Something's not right."

Before Torin could respond, the shadows surged outward, tendrils of darkness lashing through the air. They wrapped around Aria, pulling her forward with an unnatural strength. Torin lunged after her, his blade flashing, but the shadows twisted around him, forming a barrier that sent him staggering back.

"Aria!" he shouted, his voice muffled as the darkness swallowed her whole.

The world went black.

Aria blinked, her surroundings shifting into focus. She was no longer at the Nexus. Instead, she stood in the center of the Verdant Clans' camp. The firelight danced warmly, the voices of the clansfolk carrying through the air, light and carefree.

But something was off.

She turned in a slow circle, her heart pounding. The scene was too perfect, too still, as though it were frozen in time. When she called out, her voice seemed to vanish into the air, unheard by the people around her. Then, she saw Torin.

He stood near the fire, speaking with Khoran and Kaela. His posture was relaxed, his expression calm—but when Aria called his name, he didn't respond. Instead, he turned toward Eira, who approached with a sly smile. The two exchanged a quiet word before Eira handed him something—a blade, dark and jagged, its surface pulsing with a faint red light.

"No," Aria whispered, her stomach twisting. "That's not right. Torin would never—"

"You don't know that," a voice hissed in her ear. She spun around, but no one was there.

The camp shifted again, the firelight dimming. Torin raised the blade, and the clansfolk around him fell silent, their eyes narrowing as they turned to Aria. She took a step back, her chest tightening.

"She's the ruin," Eira said, her voice loud and sharp. "She's the reason the rifts are spreading."

"She brought Morvan's wrath to us," Khoran growled. "She's the Shattered Queen reborn—and she'll destroy us all."

"No!" Aria shouted, but her voice was drowned out by the rising murmurs of the crowd. They closed in around her, their faces contorted with anger and fear. Even Kaela, who had always been one of her strongest allies, looked at her with cold disdain.

Torin's gaze met hers, and for a brief moment, she thought she saw a flicker of hesitation. But then he turned away, stepping to Eira's side. "We trusted you," he said, his voice low but cutting. "And you betrayed us."

"I didn't," she said, her voice trembling. "I'm trying to save you."

"You failed," the voice hissed again, echoing through the air. "You always fail."

Aria dropped to her knees, her hands pressed to her ears. "This isn't real," she muttered. "It's not real."

The scene dissolved, the shadows swirling around her again. This time, she found herself back in her own world—her home. The warm, familiar streets of her village stretched out before her, but they were empty, the air thick with an unnatural stillness.

"No," she whispered, her voice breaking. "Not here."

The shadows moved, forming into shapes—her family, her friends. But their faces were blank, their voices absent. They turned to her, their hollow eyes accusing.

"You left us," one of them said, their voice a distorted echo of her own. "You abandoned everything."

"I didn't have a choice!" she cried, stepping back. "I didn't—"

"You'll abandon them too," the voice continued, relentless. "The clans, Torin—they'll fall because of you."

The weight of the words crushed her, threatening to drag her down into the shadows. But as the darkness closed in, something inside her pushed back—a spark of defiance.

"No," she said, her voice steadying. "This isn't real. This is Morvan's doing."

The shadows hissed, recoiling slightly, but they didn't dissipate.

"You think you can stop me?" a new voice rumbled, low and cold. The shadows coalesced into a towering figure, its glowing red eyes burning into hers. "You are nothing. A broken queen trying to save a broken world."

Aria's chest heaved, but she forced herself to stand. "I may be broken," she said, her voice firm, "but I'm not alone."

The figure laughed, a deep, mocking sound. "Then show me your strength, little queen."

The shadows surged forward, but this time, Aria didn't back down. She reached for the essence within her, the shadow power she had claimed in the Hall of Echoes. It flared to life, bright and sharp, slicing through the illusions like a blade. The figures dissolved, their accusations fading into silence.

When the darkness finally receded, she found herself back at the Nexus. Torin was at her side, his hand gripping her arm as he shouted her name. The barrier of shadows had disappeared, leaving the two of them alone in the eerie stillness.

"Aria," Torin said, his voice rough with worry. "What happened? You were—"

"I'm fine," she said quickly, though her voice shook. She looked at him, relief washing over her at the sight of his familiar face. "It was Morvan. He tried to—he showed me things."

Torin's grip on her arm tightened. "You're safe now."

She nodded, though the lingering fear in her chest told her otherwise. The illusions may have been broken, but Morvan's message was clear—this fight was far from over.

The darkness writhed around Aria like a living thing, its tendrils twisting and clawing at her mind. She stumbled through the void, her breaths ragged, her resolve fraying. Every step felt heavier than the last, each shadow whispering doubts that gnawed at her heart.

"You can't save them," the voices hissed, overlapping like a chorus of venomous truths. "You'll fail, just as you've failed before."

"No," Aria whispered, her voice trembling but defiant. "This isn't real."

The shadows pressed closer, forming grotesque shapes that loomed over her, their hollow eyes glowing faintly. "Isn't it? How many have you already lost? How many more will fall because of you?"

Aria faltered, the weight of their accusations pulling her to her knees. Her fingers clawed at the cold, featureless ground, her chest tightening as the whispers grew louder. Memories twisted into nightmares played out before her—her family turning away in disappointment, the clans falling to ruin, Torin standing with Eira, his gaze filled with betrayal.

"Stop it!" she shouted, her voice breaking. "This isn't real!"

"But it could be," the shadows purred, circling her. "You doubt yourself. We see it. And they see it too."

The world around her seemed to shrink, the oppressive darkness closing in until she could barely breathe. Her hands trembled as she pressed them to her ears, trying to block out the whispers, but they slithered into her mind like oil.

Then, faintly, cutting through the suffocating gloom, she heard it.

"Aria!" Torin's voice rang out, clear and strong.

Her head snapped up, her heart skipping a beat. "Torin?" she whispered, her voice barely audible.

"Aria!" His voice came again, insistent, urgent. It was like a lifeline, pulling her from the depths of despair. "Don't let them win. You're stronger than this."

The shadows hissed, their shapes twisting with rage. "He cannot save you. No one can."

Aria's hands clenched into fists, her trembling subsiding as she focused on the sound of Torin's voice. "He doesn't have to save me," she said, her voice growing steadier. "Because I'm not giving up."

She forced herself to stand, her legs shaking but firm beneath her. The shadows swirled angrily, their whispers rising to a deafening roar. But Torin's voice cut through the chaos, grounding her.

"Fight, Aria!" he called. "You can do this. I'm with you."

She closed her eyes, reaching deep within herself, searching for the essence she had claimed in the Hall of Echoes. It flickered faintly at first, like the dying embers of a fire, but as she focused, it flared to life, warm and steady.

The shadows recoiled, their shapes distorting as the light within her grew brighter. "You are nothing!" they shrieked, their voices desperate. "You will fail!"

"No," Aria said, opening her eyes. They glowed faintly, the essence burning within her. "I'm not nothing. And I'm not afraid of you."

The light erupted from her in a brilliant wave, pushing the shadows back. They screamed, their forms disintegrating into wisps of smoke. The void trembled, the oppressive weight lifting as the last of the darkness dissolved.

When the illusion finally broke, Aria found herself kneeling at the edge of the Nexus. The cold stone beneath her hands was real, solid, and reassuring. Her breaths came in gasps, her heart pounding as she tried to steady herself.

"Aria!" Torin was at her side in an instant, his hands gripping her shoulders as he pulled her upright. "Are you okay? What happened?"

She looked up at him, her vision clearing. His face was etched with worry, his dark eyes searching hers for answers. "I—" she began, her voice hoarse. "It was Morvan. He tried to break me."

Torin's jaw tightened, his grip on her shoulders firm. "But he didn't."

"No," she said, her voice stronger now. "He didn't."

Torin exhaled, relief flashing across his face. "I thought I'd lost you."

"You didn't," Aria said, her gaze steady. "And I won't let him win."

She stood on her own, brushing herself off as she turned back to the Nexus. The swirling energy within it no longer seemed as overwhelming. Instead, it felt… manageable. She could feel the power of the essence within her, a steady pulse that matched her own heartbeat.

"What now?" Torin asked, his voice quieter.

Aria looked at him, a flicker of determination in her eyes. "Now, we finish this."

She reached for his hand, her grip firm. Together, they faced the Nexus, its dark energy no longer a source of fear but a challenge to be overcome. For the first time, Aria felt the clarity she had been searching for—the purpose she had doubted but now fully embraced.

Whatever lay ahead, she was ready.

The swirling shadows of the Nexus seemed to settle, the chaotic tendrils withdrawing as if sensing Aria's newfound strength. She stood at the edge of the vortex, her staff glowing faintly with the essence she had claimed, her breaths steadying after the harrowing ordeal. Beside her, Torin's presence was a steady anchor, his hand resting lightly on the hilt of his blade as his dark eyes scanned the shifting darkness.

For a moment, neither of them spoke. The weight of what had just transpired hung heavily in the air, the echoes of Morvan's manipulation still lingering in Aria's mind. She exhaled slowly, her voice breaking the silence.

"He tried to break me," she said softly, her gaze fixed on the Nexus. "To make me believe I wasn't enough. That I'd fail."

Torin turned to her, his expression unreadable but his voice steady. "But you didn't. You're still here."

"Because of you," she admitted, meeting his gaze. "I heard your voice. It was the only thing that felt real."

Torin's lips pressed into a thin line, and for a moment, he said nothing. Then, his voice softened. "You've always been strong, Aria. Morvan's games didn't show you anything I didn't already know you could overcome."

Her chest tightened at his words, a quiet warmth spreading through her. "It didn't feel that way," she said. "It felt like everything I've been fighting for was slipping through my fingers. Like… I was alone."

"You're not," Torin said firmly, stepping closer. "Not now. Not ever."

Aria looked at him, her resolve hardening. "We have to stop him, Torin. Morvan isn't just using the shadows to destroy Ilyria—he's trying to break us from the inside out. If he succeeds…" She trailed off, the weight of her fears unspoken but clear.

"He won't," Torin said, his voice low but fierce. "We won't let him."

She nodded, her fingers tightening around the staff. The glow of the runes seemed to pulse in response, as though sensing her renewed determination. "This isn't just about the prophecy anymore," she said. "It's about all of us. The clans, the Shamans, the people who've been fighting for so long… They deserve more than this."

"They deserve a future," Torin agreed. He glanced at the Nexus, its dark energy swirling like a storm. "And we're going to give it to them. Together."

Aria hesitated for a moment, then reached out, her hand resting lightly on his arm. "Thank you," she said quietly. "For being here. For believing in me, even when I didn't believe in myself."

Torin's gaze softened, his usual stoic demeanor giving way to something warmer. "You make it easy," he said simply.

A faint smile tugged at her lips, the tension between them easing for the first time in what felt like days. But the moment was short-lived as the Nexus pulsed, a low hum vibrating through the air. The energy within it seemed to stir, the shadows twisting and coiling as if preparing for something.

"We don't have much time," Aria said, her tone sharpening. "The Nexus is changing. If Morvan's tied to this, then he'll know we're here."

"Let him know," Torin said, his hand moving to grip his blade. "We're not running anymore."

She looked at him, the determination in his eyes matching her own. "No," she agreed. "We're not."

As they turned to face the swirling energy together, the faint glow of Aria's staff grew brighter, illuminating the path ahead. For the first time since her arrival in Ilyria, she felt a sense of clarity, of purpose that transcended the prophecy. This wasn't just about fulfilling a destiny—it was about defying the darkness that had gripped this world for so long.

"Whatever happens," Aria said, her voice steady, "we end this. No more running, no more fear."

Torin nodded, his voice firm. "We fight. For Ilyria. For each other."

The connection between them felt unbreakable, a shared resolve that no shadow or illusion could fracture. Together, they stepped closer to the edge of the Nexus, the swirling darkness a challenge they were ready to face.

Morvan's tyranny had cast its shadow over Ilyria for too long. But Aria and Torin were no longer afraid of the dark. They would fight, they would endure, and they would prevail—together.

Chapter 12
Divided Hearts

The air within the Obsidian Nexus was dense with power, the swirling energy casting eerie shadows across the walls of the cavern. Aria held her staff tightly, its glowing runes pulsing faintly in rhythm with the vibrations underfoot. Torin was beside her, his sword drawn, his gaze scanning their surroundings for any sign of danger. Behind them, Kaela and a handful of their most loyal allies moved cautiously, their faces a mixture of awe and apprehension.

At the center of the cavern, a pedestal carved from the same jagged black stone as the walls stood beneath the pulsing vortex of shadow and light. On it rested a shard of crystal, its surface jagged and dark but glimmering faintly with an inner light. Aria knew instantly—this was it, the final fragment.

"There," Kaela said, her voice hushed but urgent. "That has to be it."

Torin nodded, his voice steady. "Stay alert. Morvan wouldn't leave something like this unguarded."

Aria stepped forward, her heart pounding as the fragment seemed to call to her. Each step felt heavier, the energy in the room pressing down on her like a weight. "It's the last piece," she murmured, her fingers brushing the edge of the pedestal. "The prophecy…"

"Careful," Torin said, his tone edged with concern. "We don't know what it'll do."

"I don't think it's dangerous," Aria replied, though her voice lacked conviction. She hesitated for a moment before reaching out, her fingers closing around the fragment.

The moment she touched it, the world around her shifted.

The cavern dissolved into blinding light, and Aria found herself standing in a vast, empty space. The air was warm, filled with the faint hum of energy. Ahead of her stood Maelis, the Shattered Queen, her presence regal and commanding. Her violet eyes burned with an intensity that made Aria feel small but not unwelcome.

"Aria," Maelis said, her voice like a melody woven with steel. "You have come far."

Aria swallowed hard, her fingers still clutching the fragment. "You—this is your prophecy. Your fight. I don't understand it."

Maelis inclined her head, her expression both kind and solemn. "The prophecy was never meant to bind you. It is a guide, not a chain."

"But why me?" Aria asked, her voice trembling. "I'm no one. I wasn't supposed to be here."

"You are exactly who you are meant to be," Maelis replied. "The essence does not choose lightly. You carry within you the strength to bridge the broken, to unite what has been fractured."

"The clans… the rifts…" Aria began, her thoughts racing. "I've tried, but they don't trust me. Some of them think I'm the ruin."

"The ruin and the salvation are two sides of the same coin," Maelis said, stepping closer. "Ilyria's future rests not on power, but on unity. The essence connects all things. It is not yours to wield alone—it is a thread that must bind you to others."

Aria frowned, her grip tightening on the fragment. "But what if I fail? What if I can't hold them together?"

Maelis's gaze softened. "Failure is not in trying, Aria. It is in surrendering to fear. You are not alone in this. You never have been."

Before Aria could respond, the vision shifted. The light around her fractured, revealing images—Torin standing at her side, the clans rallying together, the rifts closing, and, at the heart of it all, a great darkness that loomed over the land. The final image was of herself, standing with her allies, her staff raised high, the essence flowing through her like a river of light.

"This is your path," Maelis said. "Not predetermined, but chosen. Trust in yourself, and in those who stand beside you."

Aria gasped as the vision faded, the weight of the fragment in her hand grounding her. She was back in the Nexus, the shadows still swirling but the energy somehow calmer, less chaotic. Torin's hand was on her arm, steadying her, his dark eyes searching hers.

"Aria," he said, his voice low. "What did you see?"

She looked at him, her heart pounding but her mind clearer than it had been in weeks. "I saw her," she said softly. "Maelis. She showed me… everything. The prophecy, the essence—it's about more than power. It's about connection. Unity."

Kaela stepped closer, her spear in hand. "Unity? That's what this has all been about?"

Aria nodded, turning to face the group. "The essence isn't just a tool. It's a thread that binds us. All of us. The clans, the Shamans, even the land itself. If we don't stand together, we lose everything."

Torin's gaze softened, his voice steady. "Then we make them see it. Whatever it takes."

Aria met his eyes, a flicker of gratitude passing between them. "We will," she said, her voice firm. "We don't have a choice."

Kaela smirked faintly, her green eyes glinting. "Well, you've got my spear. Let's see if the others are smart enough to follow."

Aria smiled despite the weight of what lay ahead. The path was clear now, and though the challenges were far from over, she felt a sense of purpose that could not be shaken.

The final fragment was theirs. And with it, the fight for Ilyria's future had truly begun.

The fragment in Aria's hand pulsed with a steady rhythm, its glow illuminating her surroundings. She stood once more in the vast, glowing space of her vision, the warmth of the light contrasting sharply with the cold darkness of the Nexus she'd left behind. Ahead of her, Maelis appeared again, her form more defined, her presence a mixture of power and sorrow.

"Maelis," Aria said, her voice trembling with both awe and urgency. "You keep showing me pieces of this, but I don't know how to fix it. I don't know if I can."

Maelis stepped closer, her violet eyes meeting Aria's. "The burden you carry is not one of answers, Aria. It is one of choice."

"Choice?" Aria repeated, confusion tightening her chest. "The prophecy says I'm supposed to stop Morvan. That I'm supposed to—"

"The prophecy guides," Maelis interrupted, her tone gentle but firm. "It does not command. Prophecies are threads, woven into the fabric of the world. They are not chains."

Aria hesitated, her grip tightening on the glowing fragment. "But what if I make the wrong choice? What if I fail?"

Maelis extended her hand, brushing her fingers against Aria's cheek. The touch was warm, grounding. "Failure is not in the choice itself. It is in the fear that keeps you from acting."

Aria blinked, her vision blurring as the weight of Maelis's words settled over her. "Then what am I supposed to do? How do I stop Morvan? How do I fix the rifts?"

"The rifts are the scars of division," Maelis said, her voice soft but filled with a quiet power. "They were born of greed, fear, and isolation. Morvan exploited them, but their roots lie in the breaking of unity. Only through selflessness can they be healed."

"Selflessness," Aria repeated, her heart sinking. "But how? The clans can't even trust each other, let alone me. Morvan feeds on that division, and I can't stop him alone."

"You are not alone," Maelis said, her tone soothing. "You never have been."

The space around them shifted, revealing images of Torin standing steadfast beside her, Kaela rallying the clans, the Shamans bowing in reverence. Each face was a reminder of the connections she'd forged, the allies who had chosen to fight alongside her.

"The essence connects all things," Maelis continued. "It is not a weapon to wield, but a bond to strengthen. Power alone will not save Ilyria. Only unity can."

Aria's grip on the fragment loosened as the realization settled in. "It's not about defeating him with force," she murmured. "It's about bringing everyone together. Showing them there's more to fight for than just survival."

Maelis nodded, her expression softening. "The curse will not break through violence. It will break when the rifts within hearts are healed. When fear is replaced by trust, and power is tempered by sacrifice."

Aria's chest tightened. "Sacrifice," she whispered. "What kind of sacrifice?"

Maelis didn't answer immediately. Instead, she stepped back, her form beginning to flicker. "Your path is your own, Aria. The choices you make will shape not only your destiny but the fate of Ilyria. Trust in yourself, and in those who stand beside you."

"Wait," Aria said, stepping forward. "I still don't understand. What if I—"

Maelis's voice echoed as her form began to fade, her presence like a warm breeze slipping through Aria's fingers. "You are stronger than you know, Aria. Believe in the light within you—and the light in others."

The vision dissolved, leaving Aria standing alone in the Nexus once more. The fragment in her hand pulsed one final time before settling, its glow dimming but its energy steady. She exhaled, her breath shaky as the weight of Maelis's words sank in.

Torin's voice broke through the silence. "Aria." He stepped closer, his gaze searching hers. "What did she say?"

"She… she said it's not about power," Aria replied, her voice quiet but steady. "It's about unity. About sacrifice."

Torin frowned, his brow furrowing. "Sacrifice? What does that mean?"

"I'm not sure," Aria admitted, her fingers tightening around the fragment. "But I know one thing. If we're going to end this, we can't do it alone. The clans, the Shamans, everyone—they have to stand together. That's the only way."

Torin nodded, his expression resolute. "Then we make them see it. Whatever it takes."

Aria met his gaze, a flicker of hope sparking in her chest despite the uncertainty that loomed ahead. "Whatever it takes," she echoed.

As the swirling energy of the Nexus hummed around them, Aria felt a renewed sense of purpose. Maelis's final words weren't just a message—they were a call to action. The path forward was steep and uncertain, but it was no longer hers to walk alone. Together, they would find a way to heal Ilyria, one choice at a time.

The swirling energies of the Obsidian Nexus had quieted, leaving an almost eerie stillness in the cavern. The faint hum of the essence still vibrated through the air, but it was softer now, like the breath of a great beast that had finally been tamed. Aria stood near the pedestal, the fragment in her hands glowing faintly. Its pulse matched her heartbeat, steady and slow, grounding her as her thoughts raced.

She turned the fragment over in her hands, its surface jagged and cold. Yet it seemed alive, humming with a power she could feel but not fully grasp. The weight of Maelis's words hung heavily over her, each syllable echoing in her mind. Unity. Sacrifice. Trust.

Aria exhaled and looked up, her gaze drifting over the jagged walls of the cavern. The responsibility she now carried felt immeasurable, like she was standing at the edge of an abyss with no clear way across. For so long, she had doubted herself—her place in this world, her ability to live up to the prophecy, her strength to lead. And now, even with Maelis's guidance, the path forward felt overwhelming.

Torin's voice cut through her thoughts, low and steady. "You're quiet."

She turned to find him standing a few steps away, his arms crossed and his dark eyes watching her closely. His posture was relaxed, but the tension in his expression betrayed his concern.

"I'm just… thinking," Aria said, her voice soft.

"About what?"

"Everything," she admitted. She gestured to the fragment in her hand. "What Maelis said. What it means. What happens next."

Torin stepped closer, his boots crunching softly against the stone floor. "And?"

Aria let out a humorless laugh, shaking her head. "And it feels like too much. Like I'm supposed to solve every problem, heal every rift, stop Morvan, and somehow make everyone believe in me—all at once."

Torin tilted his head slightly, studying her. "You've done more than anyone else would have, Aria. If anyone can do this, it's you."

"That's the thing," she said, meeting his gaze. "I don't think I can do it alone. And I don't know if I can get everyone to stand together. The clans barely trust me. Some of them still think I'm the ruin, Torin. How am I supposed to convince them that unity is the answer?"

"You're not," he said simply.

She blinked, caught off guard. "What?"

"You're not supposed to convince them," Torin said. "You're supposed to lead them. And if they don't follow, that's their choice. But you can't let their doubt stop you from doing what you know is right."

Aria stared at him, his words sinking in. "Lead them," she repeated, her voice quieter. "Even if they don't believe in me."

Torin nodded. "Belief isn't always instant. Sometimes it takes time. But you've already earned the loyalty of the Shamans, Kaela, and others. That's a start."

A faint smile tugged at her lips, though it didn't quite reach her eyes. "When did you become so wise?"

He smirked, the corner of his mouth quirking up. "It comes and goes."

Her smile faded as her gaze returned to the fragment. "What if I make the wrong choice? What if I fail?"

"You won't," he said, his voice firm.

"You don't know that," she replied, her tone edged with uncertainty.

"I don't need to," Torin said, his expression softening. "Because I trust you."

The sincerity in his voice made her chest tighten, and for a moment, the weight of her doubts eased. She looked at him, the steady presence that had been with her through every step of this journey, and felt a flicker of hope.

"Thank you," she said quietly. "For always being here. For believing in me."

"You don't have to thank me," Torin replied. "This fight is as much mine as it is yours."

She nodded, her resolve hardening. The responsibility still loomed large, but it no longer felt insurmountable. Maelis's words weren't a warning—they were a guide, a reminder that the fight ahead wasn't hers to face alone. The essence wasn't just hers to wield; it was a bond, a connection that tied her to everyone around her.

"I'll do it," Aria said, her voice steady now. "I'll find a way to bring them together. To end this, once and for all."

Torin's lips twitched into a faint smile. "Good. Because I'm not letting you back out now."

She laughed softly, the sound breaking through the tension in the air. For the first time in what felt like days, she felt a sense of clarity. The path ahead was still uncertain, but she was no longer afraid to walk it.

With the fragment glowing faintly in her hand, Aria turned to face the swirling energy of the Nexus. The immense power within it no longer felt like a threat but a challenge—a challenge she was ready to meet.

"Let's go," she said, her voice firm.

Torin nodded, falling into step beside her as they moved forward together. Whatever lay ahead, Aria knew she wasn't walking into it alone. Together, they would face the darkness—and they would prevail.

The cavern pulsed with energy, the air thick with the weight of something ancient and powerful. The Obsidian Nexus shimmered before Aria, its swirling shadows now streaked with brilliant veins of light. The fragment in her hand grew warm, almost alive, its glow matching the hum that resonated deep within her chest. She took a step forward, each movement deliberate, as though crossing an invisible threshold.

Torin stood at her side, his hand resting lightly on the hilt of his blade, his gaze steady. Kaela and the others lingered at the edges of the room, their expressions a mixture of awe and apprehension. They were all waiting—for her.

"Aria," Torin said quietly, his voice breaking the heavy silence. "This is it."

She nodded, her grip tightening on the fragment. "It feels… different. Like it's calling to me."

"It should," Kaela said, her tone uncharacteristically serious. "That thing's tied to the essence, isn't it? To you. If the prophecy's real, this is where it all comes together."

Aria glanced down at the fragment, its glow reflecting in her eyes. "But what if I'm not ready? What if I can't handle it?"

"You're ready," Torin said firmly. "You've proven it every step of the way."

Kaela snorted, her sharp voice cutting through the tension. "Yeah, and if you're not, we're all screwed anyway, so might as well go for it."

Despite herself, Aria smiled faintly. "Thanks for the vote of confidence."

Torin stepped closer, his voice softening. "You've come this far, Aria. Maelis chose you for a reason. The essence chose you. Trust that. And trust yourself."

She met his gaze, his unwavering belief in her steadying the storm of doubt swirling in her chest. "I'll try," she said, her voice quieter now.

"Don't just try," Torin said, his expression serious. "Do it."

Taking a deep breath, Aria turned back to the Nexus. The energy within it seemed to respond to her, the light and shadows shifting, drawing her closer. She lifted the fragment, its glow intensifying until it was almost blinding. The air around her grew warmer, crackling with an electric charge.

"This is it," she whispered, more to herself than anyone else.

Torin's voice was calm but resolute. "We're with you."

Aria stepped forward, the fragment in her hand seeming to pull her toward the heart of the Nexus. As she crossed the final distance, the swirling energy enveloped her, wrapping around her like a second skin. The light and shadows fused together, flowing into her body, filling every inch of her with a power that was both overwhelming and exhilarating.

She cried out, her voice echoing through the cavern as the essence surged through her. Memories not her own flashed behind her eyes—visions of Maelis, of battles fought and sacrifices made, of the essence being forged into a tool of unity and strength. She saw the rifts tearing through Ilyria, felt the pain of its people, and understood the weight of the prophecy in a way she never had before.

"Aria!" Torin's voice reached her, cutting through the chaos in her mind.

"I'm fine," she managed, though her voice trembled. "I think… I think it's working."

Her body glowed with a radiant light, the essence flowing through her in waves. She could feel it—fire, water, air, earth, shadow—all the elements of the essence blending seamlessly within her. For the first time, she understood the full power of the Shattered Queen's Mantle.

"What's happening?" Kaela asked, her voice edged with awe.

"She's accepting it," Torin said, his gaze never leaving Aria. "She's becoming what the prophecy always said she would be."

Aria opened her eyes, the glowing runes on her staff flaring to life. Her voice was steady now, filled with a confidence she hadn't known she possessed. "I understand now. The essence… it's not about control. It's about balance. Unity."

Kaela let out a low whistle. "Well, you certainly look the part of a prophecy's chosen one."

Aria turned to Torin, her glowing eyes meeting his. "I can feel it, Torin. All of it. The power, the connection… the responsibility. It's so much."

"You don't have to bear it alone," he said softly. "We're with you."

She nodded, her grip on the staff firm. "I know. And that's the only reason I can do this."

As the light around her began to settle, Aria felt a sense of clarity she'd never known before. The path ahead was still dangerous, still uncertain, but she no longer doubted her place on it. The Shattered Queen's Mantle wasn't a burden—it was a promise. A promise she intended to keep.

"We move forward," she said, her voice resonating through the cavern. "Together."

Chapter 13
The Weight of Leadership

The jungle's unrelenting humidity clung to Aria like a second skin, every step through the dense foliage draining what little patience she had left. She pushed a low-hanging branch out of her way, muttering under her breath as her boots sank into the damp ground. Ahead of her, Torin moved with his usual steady efficiency, his blade slicing through the overgrowth without hesitation.

"How are you not tired?" she snapped, her voice sharper than she intended.

Torin glanced over his shoulder but didn't stop. "I've been doing this my whole life. You get used to it."

"Well, I haven't been doing this my whole life," she retorted, shoving another branch aside. "I've been dragged into it, and honestly, I'm starting to think I'm in over my head."

Torin slowed, finally turning to face her. His expression was calm but edged with irritation. "You've been saying that since the start, and yet you're still here."

"Because I don't have a choice," she shot back. "Or did you forget that part? Everyone's putting their hopes on me, but no one's bothering to tell me anything useful."

He raised an eyebrow. "What do you want to know?"

"Oh, I don't know," she said, throwing her hands up. "Maybe what we're walking into next? Or what else the prophecy says about me? You've been with me this whole time, and it feels like you know a hell of a lot more than you're letting on."

Torin's jaw tightened. "And what makes you think you're ready to hear it?"

Her eyes widened in disbelief. "Are you serious right now? I'm supposed to save the world, remember? If there's something I need to know, you'd better tell me."

He took a step closer, his gaze steady and unyielding. "You think it's that simple? That knowing more will make this easier for you? It won't. If anything, it'll make it harder."

"Harder than this?" she demanded, gesturing to the tangled jungle around them. "Harder than carrying the weight of an entire prophecy on my shoulders? What could possibly be worse than that?"

"You don't know what you're asking for," he said, his voice low. "The truth isn't just answers, Aria. It's choices. And once you know them, you can't go back."

"Maybe I don't want to go back," she said, stepping closer. "Maybe I just want to stop feeling like I'm stumbling through this blind while everyone else expects me to fix their mess."

Torin's expression darkened, his voice sharp. "Then stop acting like a victim and start taking responsibility."

Her breath caught, her anger flaring. "I didn't ask for this!"

"And yet here you are," he snapped. "You think I wanted this either? To spend my days protecting someone who's too scared to step up? This isn't about what we want, Aria. It's about what's needed."

She stared at him, her chest rising and falling as her frustration warred with the sting of his words. "You don't know what it's like," she said quietly, her voice trembling. "To have everyone look at you like you're some kind of savior when you don't even know if you believe in yourself."

Torin's expression softened slightly, though his voice remained firm. "You think I don't know what it's like to carry a burden you didn't choose? I lost my home, my family—everything—because of these rifts. Do you think I get to walk away from that?"

Her shoulders slumped, her anger faltering as she searched his face. "Torin, I..."

"No," he interrupted, his tone gentler now. "You're right about one thing. I've been holding back. But not because I don't trust you. Because I know how heavy this is, and once you understand it, there's no going back."

She looked away, her hands clenching into fists. "I don't want to fail."

"Then don't," he said simply. "You don't have to have all the answers right now. But you need to start trusting yourself. The villagers, the elders—they see something in you. Maybe it's time you start seeing it too."

Aria let out a shaky breath, her anger replaced by a gnawing uncertainty. "I don't even know where to start."

Torin stepped back, his voice steady but not unkind. "You've already started. Every step you take, every choice you make—it's all part of it. Stop waiting for someone else to tell you what to do."

She nodded slowly, her gaze meeting his. "Fine. But if I'm doing this, I need you to stop treating me like a liability."

Torin allowed a faint smirk, though his eyes remained serious. "Then stop acting like one."

Her lips twitched into a reluctant smile, the tension between them easing slightly. "You're impossible, you know that?"

"I've been told," he said, turning back to the path. "Now let's keep moving. The rifts won't wait for us to figure this out."

As they continued their journey, the air between them felt less charged, their unspoken truce carrying them forward. For the first time, Aria felt a glimmer of something she hadn't allowed herself before—resolve. She might not have all the answers, but she was still standing. And that, she realized, was a start.

The jungle was quiet now, the distant hum of nocturnal creatures creating a soothing rhythm against the crackle of the campfire. The flames danced lazily, casting flickering shadows across Torin's face as he sat cross-legged a few feet away from Aria. His blade rested nearby, always within arm's reach, though his posture was more relaxed than usual. He stared into the fire, his expression distant, the lines of his face softened by the warm light.

Aria watched him from her seat on a flat stone, her fingers absently tracing the edge of her blanket. The tension between them from earlier had faded, replaced by a lingering silence that felt heavier than it should have. She wanted to say something, anything, but the weight of the day hung over her like a storm cloud.

"You're quiet tonight," she said finally, her voice gentle but curious.

Torin didn't look at her. "Long day."

"You're always quiet," she said, a faint smile tugging at her lips. "But this is... different."

He exhaled slowly, leaning forward to rest his elbows on his knees. "Just thinking."

"About?" she pressed, tilting her head.

For a moment, she thought he wouldn't answer. But then he shifted slightly, his gaze still fixed on the fire. "The prophecy. The rifts. My people."

"Your people?" Aria asked, sitting up straighter. "You've never really talked about them before."

Torin hesitated, his jaw tightening briefly before he spoke. "There's not much to talk about. They're gone."

She blinked, caught off guard by the rawness in his voice. "Gone? You mean...?"

"Most of them," he said quietly. "My village was one of the first to fall to the rifts. We were too close to the borderlands, too isolated to get help. By the time anyone realized what was happening, it was already over."

"Torin..." she began, her voice soft.

He shook his head, cutting her off. "It wasn't just the rifts. The tribes—their refusal to work together, their constant fighting—it left us vulnerable. The rifts didn't just destroy my home; they exposed how broken we've become as a people."

Aria's chest tightened as she listened, the weight of his words settling heavily over her. "And that's why you're so invested in the prophecy," she said quietly. "Because it's the only way to fix what's broken."

Torin's lips pressed into a thin line. "I want to believe it is. I want to believe that if we find the fragments, if we stop the rifts, we can put things back together. But..."

"But what?" she prompted, leaning closer.

He finally looked at her, his dark eyes shadowed with something she hadn't seen before—doubt. "What if it's not enough? What if we're too far gone? The prophecy might be real, but the tribes... they've spent so long fighting each other, I don't know if they can come back from it."

Aria felt a pang of sympathy as she met his gaze. He always carried himself with such unshakable confidence, but now, she saw the cracks beneath the surface. He wasn't just a warrior; he was someone who had lost everything and was clinging to the only thread of hope left.

"You're not the only one doubting all of this, you know," she said, her voice softer now. "I've been questioning it since the day I touched that shard. But... I don't think that makes us weak. I think it means we care."

Torin raised an eyebrow. "You think doubt is a strength?"

"I think it's human," she replied. "And you're a lot more human than you let on."

A faint smirk tugged at his lips, though it didn't quite reach his eyes. "Careful, Aria. You're starting to sound like you might actually believe in me."

She laughed softly, the tension between them easing slightly. "I think you're easier to believe in than some ancient prophecy."

"Flattering," he said dryly, though there was a trace of warmth in his tone. He leaned back, his gaze returning to the fire. "I just wish I could do more. For my people. For this world."

"You already are," she said firmly. "You're here, helping me when you could have walked away. That's more than most would do."

Torin was quiet for a long moment, his expression unreadable. Then he gave a small nod. "Maybe. But it still doesn't feel like enough."

"It's a start," Aria said, offering him a faint smile. "And right now, that's all we've got."

He looked at her again, his gaze softer this time. "You're stronger than you think, you know."

She chuckled, shaking her head. "Coming from you, that's practically a compliment."

"Don't get used to it," he replied, but the corner of his mouth lifted in a ghost of a smile.

The silence that followed wasn't heavy this time. It felt lighter, more comfortable, as if the air between them had shifted. Aria leaned back against the stone, the warmth of the fire soothing her frayed nerves. For the first time in days, she felt a flicker of something she hadn't allowed herself to feel—hope.

And though Torin still carried his doubts, she saw something else in him now—a man fighting not just for survival, but for redemption.

The tension in the air was palpable as Aria stepped into the clearing, the eyes of the tribe fixed on her like predators sizing up prey. The warriors of the Red Thorn clan stood in a semicircle around her, their faces painted with vivid streaks of red and black. Spears rested lightly in their hands, their sharp tips glinting in the fading light.

Torin moved to stand just behind her, his posture rigid, his hand hovering near his blade. "Careful," he murmured under his breath. "They're not convinced you're who you say you are."

"Great," Aria muttered back, her voice low but strained. "Neither am I."

One of the warriors stepped forward, taller than the others, his painted face split by a long scar that ran from his brow to his jaw. He spoke in a deep, commanding voice, the tribal dialect thick and unfamiliar. The elder accompanying them, a stooped man with gray-streaked hair, translated.

"He says you claim to be the one chosen by Seluna," the elder said, his tone careful. "But the Red Thorn does not believe in words alone. They demand proof."

Aria glanced at Torin, her heart racing. "What kind of proof are we talking about?"

Torin's expression was grim. "Essence magic. They'll want to see if it responds to you."

"Of course they will," Aria muttered, her hands clenching at her sides. She looked back at the warriors, their expressions stony, unyielding. "And what happens if it doesn't?"

"They'll take it as confirmation that you're a fraud," Torin replied flatly. "And if they think you're lying... well, the Red Thorn aren't known for mercy."

Her stomach twisted, the weight of the situation pressing heavily on her. She turned back to the warriors, forcing herself to stand taller. "I don't even know how to control it. What if I can't do what they want?"

"You've done it before," Torin said, his voice firm. "Just focus."

"Focus," she echoed, her voice shaking. "That's your advice? Focus?"

"Unless you want to run," Torin replied, his tone sharp. "But if you do, they'll chase us, and I don't think either of us wants to find out how fast they are."

She glared at him, but before she could retort, the scarred warrior barked something in his guttural language. The elder translated again.

"He says time is short. If you are Seluna's chosen, show them."

Aria swallowed hard, her heart pounding. She stepped forward hesitantly, her palms damp with sweat. The warriors watched her every move, their painted faces unreadable but their spears shifting slightly, as if preparing for the slightest provocation.

"Okay," she whispered to herself, closing her eyes. "I can do this. I have to do this."

The memory of the vines bursting from the ground during the panther attack surfaced in her mind. She tried to recall the warmth she had felt then, the raw energy that had surged through her. Her breathing steadied as she reached for that connection, her hands hovering just above the earth.

Nothing happened.

She opened one eye, peeking down at her hands. The ground remained still, the air heavy with anticipation but void of any sign of essence magic.

"Aria," Torin said under his breath, his tone edged with urgency. "They're losing patience."

"I know!" she hissed back, her voice frantic. She tried again, this time clenching her fists and focusing harder, willing the energy to come. The ground beneath her remained lifeless.

The scarred warrior barked another order, his voice louder now, laced with irritation. The elder stepped forward, his expression apologetic. "He says you are wasting their time. If you cannot prove your connection, you should leave before they force you to."

Aria's stomach twisted, her hands trembling. She turned to Torin, her voice breaking. "I can't do this. I don't even know how this is supposed to work. What if they're right? What if I'm not—"

"You are," Torin said firmly, stepping closer. "You've done it before, Aria. You've felt it. It's there. Trust it."

She shook her head, her voice rising. "You don't understand! I barely believe in this myself! How am I supposed to convince them when I can't even convince me?"

Torin's expression softened, though his tone remained steady. "Because you're stronger than you think. And because you don't have a choice."

She stared at him, her breath catching as his words sunk in. Slowly, she turned back to the scarred warrior, meeting his piercing gaze. The doubts in her chest burned like fire, but beneath them, she felt a flicker of something else—a determination she hadn't realized she possessed.

"I am Seluna's chosen," she said, her voice trembling but growing steadier with each word. "And if I can't prove that to you now, then give me time. The rifts are destroying this world. Fighting each other won't stop them. But working together might."

The warrior tilted his head, his scarred face unreadable. For a long, agonizing moment, the clearing was silent except for the rustle of leaves in the wind. Then, slowly, he raised a hand, signaling for the other warriors to lower their spears.

The elder turned to Aria, his expression a mixture of surprise and relief. "He says your words carry weight. He will give you time to prove yourself."

Aria let out a shaky breath, her legs nearly giving way beneath her. Torin stepped closer, his voice low enough that only she could hear. "That was a risk."

She glanced at him, exhaustion and determination warring in her eyes. "So is everything else in this world."

For the first time, she felt the smallest spark of belief—not in the prophecy, but in herself. And for now, that would have to be enough.

The Red Thorn tribe gathered in a wide circle around a blazing fire in the heart of their camp. The flickering flames illuminated their painted faces, the shadows dancing across their expressions of skepticism and thinly veiled distrust. Aria stood at the center, her posture stiff but steady, with Torin a few paces behind her, his presence a silent but reassuring anchor.

The scarred warrior from earlier, now seated on an elaborately carved stool, gestured toward her with a broad hand. He spoke in his native tongue, his deep voice resonating with authority. The elder translated as he stood to Aria's side.

"He says you claim to be Seluna's chosen," the elder explained. "But words are weak. To lead, you must earn trust. The Red Thorn do not bow to outsiders."

Aria swallowed hard, the weight of their expectations pressing against her. She glanced at Torin, who gave her a faint nod, his expression unreadable but his presence steady. Drawing in a slow breath, she turned back to the gathered tribe, her hands clenched at her sides.

"Trust isn't given freely," she said, her voice louder than she expected, carrying over the crackle of the fire. "And I'm not here to demand it. But your history—your ancestors—left you with something greater than distrust. They left you with the knowledge to protect this world."

The warriors murmured amongst themselves, their skepticism palpable. The scarred leader raised a hand, silencing them. He leaned forward slightly, his dark eyes narrowing as he studied her.

"You speak of knowledge," the elder translated. "But what do you know of us? Of our fight? You are not one of us."

Aria hesitated, but only for a moment. "No, I'm not," she admitted, meeting his gaze. "But I know your ancestors were the ones who stood at the borderlands when the rifts first appeared. They were the first to fight against the chaos. They created the wards that protected your lands for generations."

The murmurs grew louder this time, some of the warriors exchanging surprised glances. The elder's eyes flicked to her, his expression unreadable, but he translated her words nonetheless.

Torin stepped closer, his voice low. "Good start. Keep going."

She resisted the urge to glance back at him, instead focusing on the tribe leader. "I know this because I've studied the ruins. I've seen the carvings, the records your people left behind. They speak of strength, of unity. Your ancestors didn't fight alone. They worked with the other tribes to seal the rifts and protect Ilyria."

The leader leaned back in his seat, his expression hardening. He spoke again, his tone sharp. The elder hesitated before translating. "He says those bonds were broken long ago. The other tribes betrayed them. What strength is there in unity when it leads to ruin?"

Aria's heart pounded, but she stood her ground. "The rifts don't care about your past grudges. They'll destroy everything, Red Thorn included, unless we find a way to stop them together. And I can help. I've already felt the essence. It responds to me."

The leader's eyes narrowed further, his skepticism sharpening. He gestured for her to prove it, his movements slow and deliberate.

"You're on," Torin murmured from behind her.

Aria shot him a look before focusing on the fire. She took a deep breath, her hands stretching out toward the flames. Her connection to the essence had always been raw, unpredictable, but now she needed to trust it, to let it flow.

The warmth of the fire pulsed against her palms, and she focused on that feeling, willing it to respond. Slowly, tendrils of flame began to rise, twisting and curling unnaturally as they stretched toward her. Gasps rippled through the gathered warriors, their distrust shifting into awe as the fire danced in her hands without burning her.

She exhaled slowly, lowering her arms. The flames returned to their natural state, crackling softly once more. She turned to the tribe leader, her voice steady despite the adrenaline racing through her.

"I don't expect you to follow me blindly," she said, meeting his gaze. "But you've seen what I can do. I'm not just here to talk. I'm here to fight for Ilyria, just like your ancestors did."

The leader studied her in silence for a long moment. Then he stood, his imposing frame casting a long shadow across the fire. He spoke slowly, deliberately, and the elder translated.

"He says you have the strength to speak and the courage to act. That is enough to earn their attention—for now."

Aria felt the tension in her chest ease, though her shoulders remained stiff. "That's all I'm asking for," she said, dipping her head slightly.

The tribe began to disperse, their murmurs quieter now, their skepticism tempered by curiosity. The elder gave her a small, approving nod before following the others, leaving Aria and Torin alone by the fire.

Torin stepped closer, his arms crossed as he studied her. "You handled that well."

She let out a shaky laugh, brushing her hair back. "Well? I nearly passed out."

"Couldn't tell," he said with a faint smirk. "They saw what they needed to see. You stood your ground. That's what matters."

Aria glanced at him, the weight of the moment finally catching up with her. "I don't feel like a leader, Torin."

"Most good ones don't," he replied. "But you're getting there."

For the first time, she allowed herself a small smile. She wasn't sure if she believed in the prophecy yet, but for now, she had taken a step forward. And that was enough.

Chapter 14
The Shard of Light

The march to the Astral Nexus was silent, the unified tribes moving as one shadow under the waning moonlight. The terrain shifted as they neared their destination, the air growing heavy with the hum of magic. The trees thinned, replaced by jagged stone spires that jutted from the earth like the claws of some ancient beast. At the heart of it all stood the Astral Nexus, a swirling vortex of light and shadow suspended above a massive obsidian platform.

Aria halted the group at the edge of the clearing, her eyes locked on the figure standing at the center of the Nexus. Morvan. His presence was undeniable, the shadows coiling around him like living extensions of his malice. His dark robes billowed in the unnatural wind, and his crimson eyes gleamed with cruel anticipation.

Torin stepped to her side, his hand on the hilt of his blade. "He's waiting for us."

"Of course he is," Kaela said from behind them, her voice sharp with tension. "He's probably been planning this for centuries."

Aria tightened her grip on her staff, its essence flaring faintly in response to her unease. "That's exactly what worries me."

Khoran, ever the skeptic, crossed his arms. "So what's the plan? Charge in and hope the prophecy holds up?"

"No," Aria said firmly, turning to face the group. "We don't charge. We don't fight on his terms."

Kaela raised an eyebrow. "And what are our terms, exactly?"

Aria took a deep breath, her voice calm but resolute. "Unity. We don't let him divide us. No matter what he does, we hold the line—together."

Kaela smirked, her sharp eyes glinting. "Sounds nice on paper. Let's see how it holds up when the shadows start flying."

"She's right," Torin said, his voice steady. "If we don't stand as one, we lose before the battle even begins."

Aria nodded, her gaze sweeping over the leaders and warriors who had gathered for this final stand. "You've all fought for your people, for your clans, for survival. Tonight, we fight for Ilyria. For a future where no one has to stand alone."

The braided-haired Seris stepped forward, her expression grim but determined. "The Willowclaws are ready. Whatever happens, we'll stand."

Kaela slammed the butt of her spear against the ground. "Bloodfangs too. Let's show this shadow creep what we're made of."

Khoran hesitated, his scarred face hard. Then he sighed, his tone gruff. "Thornclaws don't back down from a fight. We'll hold."

One by one, the other leaders voiced their agreement, their resolve growing like a flame passed from torch to torch. Aria turned back to the Nexus, the swirling energy casting eerie patterns across the battlefield.

"Then let's end this," she said, her voice steady despite the storm of emotions raging within her.

They moved as one, the tribes fanning out to form a semicircle around the platform. Aria led the charge, her staff glowing brighter with each step. As they reached the edge of the Nexus, Morvan's voice rang out, cold and mocking.

"So, the Shattered Queen's successor finally arrives," he said, his tone dripping with disdain. "And you brought an army. How quaint."

Aria stepped forward, her voice cutting through the tension like a blade. "Your time is over, Morvan. The tribes are united. Ilyria won't fall to you."

Morvan laughed, the sound echoing unnaturally. "United? Is that what you call this fragile alliance? They'll turn on each other the moment I'm gone. You've built your hopes on sand, little queen."

"You're wrong," Aria said, her grip tightening on her staff. "They've chosen to fight for something bigger than themselves. That's something you'll never understand."

Morvan's crimson eyes narrowed, and the shadows around him writhed. "Brave words. Let's see if you can back them up."

With a flick of his hand, the shadows surged forward, forming grotesque shapes that leapt toward the tribes. Aria raised her staff, its light flaring as it met the darkness head-on. The first clash sent a shockwave rippling through the battlefield, the ground trembling beneath their feet.

"Hold the line!" Torin shouted, his blade flashing as he cut through a shadow beast.

Kaela let out a fierce battle cry, her spear arcing through the air to impale one of the creatures. "Come on, you ugly bastards! Is that all you've got?"

The warriors rallied, their unity holding firm as they pushed back the encroaching shadows. Aria stood at the center, her staff a beacon of light that seemed to weaken Morvan's control over the battlefield.

Morvan sneered, his voice a venomous hiss. "You think you can win? You're nothing but a flicker against the eternal dark."

Aria met his gaze, her voice unwavering. "A flicker is all it takes to start a fire."

The battle began in earnest, the tribes fighting side by side as the shadows closed in. Aria's light burned brighter, and for the first time, the Astral Nexus trembled—not with Morvan's power, but with the strength of those who dared to defy him.

The Astral Nexus erupted into chaos as Aria stepped onto the obsidian platform, her staff radiating light that clashed violently with the encroaching darkness. Morvan stood at the center, his form barely human as the shadows around him swirled like a storm. Each step she took toward him sent a pulse through the air, a ripple of light meeting the suffocating weight of his magic.

"You're bold, I'll give you that," Morvan sneered, his voice carrying a hollow, echoing resonance. "But boldness won't save you, little queen."

Aria stopped a few paces away, her staff glowing brighter with each passing second. "This isn't about saving myself," she said firmly. "It's about saving Ilyria—from you."

Morvan's laugh was low and cruel. "Save Ilyria? You're standing on its ruin, and you still don't see it. Ilyria isn't yours to save—it's mine to claim."

With a flick of his wrist, the shadows surged forward. Aria raised her staff, the light bursting outward to meet them. The clash sent a shockwave rippling through the platform, forcing her back a step. She gritted her teeth, her resolve hardening as she steadied herself.

"Is that the best you've got?" she called, her voice cutting through the din. "I thought you were supposed to be powerful."

Morvan's eyes flashed crimson, his expression twisting into something monstrous. "You dare mock me? I am power. I am eternal."

He raised both hands, the shadows rising like a tidal wave before crashing down toward her. Aria thrust her staff forward, the light expanding in a protective shield that absorbed the brunt of the attack. She staggered under the weight of his magic but held her ground.

"Eternal doesn't mean unstoppable," she shot back, her voice steady despite the strain. "And you're not as untouchable as you think."

Morvan sneered, his form shifting as the shadows swirled more violently around him. "You think your light can stand against the void? You're nothing but a flicker, destined to be snuffed out."

Aria's jaw tightened, the memories of Maelis's vision flickering in her mind. "You don't understand," she said, her voice low but filled with conviction. "This light isn't just mine. It's theirs."

Behind her, the tribes roared as they fought back the shadow beasts, their combined strength driving the creatures further from the platform. Aria could feel their unity, the essence flowing between them like a current that bolstered her own power. The realization sent a renewed surge of energy through her, and the light around her burned brighter.

"Unity," she said, her voice rising. "That's what you'll never have. That's why you'll lose."

Morvan snarled, his form flickering as if her words had struck a deeper chord. "Unity is weakness! Dependence. A chain that drags you down."

Aria met his gaze, her eyes glowing with the essence's power. "It's strength. Something you could never understand."

With a shout, she thrust her staff forward, a beam of light shooting toward Morvan. He countered with a wave of shadows, the two forces colliding in a dazzling explosion of light and dark. The ground beneath them trembled, cracks splintering through the obsidian as the clash intensified.

"You can't win!" Morvan roared, his voice a mix of fury and desperation. "You're fighting a battle that was lost centuries ago."

"I'm fighting for the future," Aria countered, her voice unwavering. "And I'm not fighting alone."

The light around her flared, pushing back the shadows as the voices of the tribes behind her rose in unison. The sound filled the air, a defiant chorus that seemed to amplify her power. Morvan recoiled, his form flickering as though the unity itself was a weapon he couldn't counter.

"You think their loyalty will save you?" he hissed, his voice venomous. "It will crumble. They'll betray you, just as they've betrayed each other."

Aria's expression hardened. "You're wrong. They've chosen to stand together. And that's something you'll never destroy."

With a final surge of energy, she channeled the essence through her staff, the light exploding outward in a brilliant wave that consumed the platform. Morvan screamed, the shadows writhing as they struggled to hold their shape. For the first time, his confidence faltered, and Aria saw the flicker of fear in his crimson eyes.

The light receded, leaving the platform cracked but intact. Morvan staggered, his form dimming, though his defiance remained. Aria took a step forward, her staff still glowing.

"This is your last chance," she said, her voice quiet but resolute. "Stand down, or we'll finish this."

Morvan's lips twisted into a snarl, his pride refusing to yield. "You don't have the strength."

Aria raised her staff, the light pulsing once more. "Watch me."

Behind her, the tribes roared again, their unity unshaken as they prepared to fight to the end. The battle was far from over, but in that moment, Aria knew they had something Morvan could never match: hope, fueled by the strength of standing together.

The obsidian platform shuddered beneath Aria's feet as Morvan's laughter echoed through the air, cold and cruel. Shadows swirled around him like living things, their tendrils lashing out and forcing Aria back. Each step felt heavier, as though the weight of the world itself conspired to crush her resolve.

"Do you feel it, little queen?" Morvan sneered, his crimson eyes glowing with malevolence. "That's the weight of your failure.

The doubts you carry. The lies you've told yourself. They're chains, and I am their master."

Aria gritted her teeth, raising her staff to block a strike of shadow magic that crashed against her like a wave. The blow sent her staggering, her knees buckling under the pressure. In the distance, she could hear the clash of steel and the shouts of her allies, but they felt distant, like echoes from another world.

"You can't win," Morvan said, his voice dripping with venom. "Your allies fight for a cause they don't even believe in. Do you think they'll follow you into the abyss? They'll abandon you, just like everyone else."

The words cut deeper than she wanted to admit. Visions of her failures rose unbidden—moments when she doubted herself, when she questioned if she was enough. The shadows twisted around her, amplifying those fears, making them feel insurmountable.

"Aria!" Torin's voice cut through the haze, sharp and steady. He stood near the edge of the platform, his blade dripping with shadow ichor. His dark eyes locked on hers, fierce with determination. "Don't listen to him. He's afraid. That's why he's doing this."

Morvan's sneer deepened, his voice softening into a mocking tone. "Afraid? Of her? She can barely stand. You should save yourself, Torin. Leave her to fall as she was always meant to."

"I'm not leaving," Torin said firmly, stepping closer to Aria. "And neither is anyone else."

Aria looked up at him, the light from her staff flickering as her strength wavered. "I… I can't—"

"Yes, you can," Torin said, his voice cutting through her doubts. "Look at them."

He gestured to the battlefield below, where warriors from every clan fought side by side, their shouts blending into a powerful roar. The Shamans chanted, their magic weaving through the air to bolster their allies. Kaela's spear flashed in the torchlight as she led a charge, her voice rising in a triumphant battle cry.

"They're here because of you," Torin said, his voice softening. "Because they believe in you. And I believe in you."

Aria's chest tightened, the weight of her fears beginning to lift. The essence within her stirred, a warmth spreading through her as she drew strength from the unity around her. She met Torin's gaze, her grip on her staff tightening.

"Thank you," she said quietly, her voice steadying.

Morvan snarled, the shadows around him surging. "Foolish sentiment! You think their belief will save you? Their hope is nothing but a flickering candle in the face of my storm."

Aria stood tall, the light from her staff growing brighter. "Hope is stronger than you think," she said. "And it's not just mine—it's all of ours."

She raised her staff, the essence within her resonating with the energy of the land itself. The ground beneath her feet glowed with faint runes, the platform responding to the unity of the tribes below. The light spread, driving back the shadows as it expanded outward.

"No!" Morvan roared, his form flickering as the light touched him. "You don't understand! The darkness is eternal! You cannot destroy it!"

"I don't need to destroy it," Aria said, her voice filled with quiet strength. "I just need to break your hold."

With a final surge of energy, she thrust her staff forward. The light exploded outward, a wave of brilliance that enveloped the Nexus and surged through the battlefield. The shadows writhed and shrieked as they were torn apart, their grip on the land severed.

Morvan let out a final, desperate scream, his form dissolving into the light. The darkness around the Nexus evaporated, leaving the air clear and still. The ground beneath them steadied, the runes fading as the energy settled.

Aria lowered her staff, her breaths ragged but her resolve unbroken. Torin stepped to her side, his hand resting lightly on her shoulder.

"You did it," he said, his voice filled with quiet awe.

"We did it," Aria corrected, a faint smile crossing her lips.

Below, the warriors began to cheer, their voices rising in a triumphant roar that echoed across the battlefield. The tribes had held together, and together, they had triumphed.

As Aria looked out over the scene, the weight of the prophecy lifted from her shoulders, replaced by the certainty that unity, not power, had won the day. This was the future she had fought for—a future built on trust, connection, and hope.

The Astral Nexus stood still, its once-swirling vortex now faded to a faint shimmer of light. The jagged obsidian platform was cracked but intact, its dark sheen softened by the glow of runes that pulsed faintly with Aria's essence. The battlefield below was quiet now, the cries of combat replaced by a stunned, reverent silence as the tribes turned their gaze upward.

At the center of it all stood Aria, her staff still raised, its light flickering like a dying ember. Her shoulders slumped as exhaustion washed over her, her legs trembling with the effort of standing. Across from her, where Morvan had once loomed, there was nothing but ash and shadows dissipating into the wind.

Torin was the first to reach her. He sheathed his blade quickly, his dark eyes scanning her face as he caught her arm to steady her. "Aria," he said, his voice low but urgent. "Are you—?"

"I'm fine," she said, though her voice was barely above a whisper. The weight of her own words betrayed her, and she swayed, the glow of her staff dimming further.

"No, you're not," Torin said firmly, his grip tightening as he supported her. "You've done enough. Let me—"

"I have to see it," she interrupted, her gaze lifting to the tribes below. Her knees buckled, and Torin caught her, lowering her carefully to the ground. Her staff clattered beside her, its runes flickering faintly as the essence within began to settle.

"Aria!" Kaela's voice carried through the clearing as she sprinted toward them, her spear streaked with the ichor of shadow beasts. She skidded to a stop, her sharp gaze raking over Aria's pale face. "What happened? Is she—?"

"She's alive," Torin said, his tone clipped. "But she needs rest."

Kaela crouched beside them, her usual smirk replaced by a rare expression of concern. "Well, that's a relief. We just took down an ancient shadow tyrant. Would've been a shame if our fearless leader didn't get to enjoy it."

Aria let out a weak laugh, though it quickly turned into a wince. "I'm... still here," she murmured. "Barely."

Kaela's grin returned, though it was softer. "Barely counts."

Below, a voice rose—a cheer, loud and clear, from one of the warriors. It was quickly followed by another, and then another, until the entire battlefield erupted in a roar of triumph. The sound swelled, carrying with it the weight of victory, the relief of survival, and the newfound hope that had taken root in their hearts.

Torin glanced down at Aria, his voice soft. "You hear that? That's for you."

"No," Aria said, shaking her head weakly. "It's for us. For Ilyria."

Kaela let out a low whistle, standing and resting her spear on her shoulder. "You've got a knack for the inspirational stuff, you know that?"

"Practice," Aria whispered, a faint smile on her lips.

The cheering grew louder as the leaders of the tribes began to ascend the platform, their expressions a mix of awe and respect. Khoran was among them, his usual scowl softened as he approached. He stopped a few paces away, his gaze flicking between Aria and the faint remnants of Morvan's darkness.

"So," he said, his voice gruff. "You actually did it."

"We did it," Aria corrected, her voice gaining strength as she pushed herself up with Torin's help. She swayed but managed to stand, her staff glowing faintly at her side. "This was never just my fight."

Khoran's expression flickered, the faintest hint of a smile breaking through. "Fair enough. But it wouldn't have happened without you."

Seris stepped forward, her braided hair streaked with blood and dirt. "He's right," she said. "You united us when no one else could. You gave us something to fight for."

Aria's chest tightened, the weight of their words both humbling and overwhelming. She met their gazes, her voice steady despite her exhaustion. "I didn't do this alone. You all chose to fight—to stand together. That's what won today. Not me. Us."

The crowd murmured in agreement, their respect for her deepening. Kaela smirked, muttering under her breath. "Modest to the end."

Torin shot her a look, his voice low. "She's earned it."

As the tribes gathered closer, the leaders began to kneel one by one, their weapons laid before them in a silent gesture of unity. The warriors followed suit, their cheers fading into a solemn reverence. Aria stood in the center of the platform, the glow of the Astral Nexus casting her in a soft light. In that moment, she wasn't just a leader or a warrior—she was the symbol of Ilyria's strength, its hope, and its future.

Her legs gave out, and Torin caught her again, his steady presence a comfort she leaned into. "You need to rest," he said softly, his voice tinged with worry.

"I know," she murmured, her eyes closing as the exhaustion finally took her. "Just... make sure they remember why we fought."

"We will," Torin promised, his voice firm. "We'll make sure they remember everything."

As the light of the Nexus faded, the tribes carried their symbol of hope to safety, their unity now unshakable. And though the cost had been great, the victory was theirs—a victory that would shape Ilyria for generations to come.

Chapter 15
Threads of Unity

The morning sun bathed the battlefield in soft golden light, revealing the scars of the battle that had nearly torn Ilyria apart. The obsidian platform of the Astral Nexus was cracked but stable, its once-imposing darkness now a faint shadow of its former self. Around it, the tribes moved with quiet purpose, the air heavy not with despair, but with determination.

Aria stood at the edge of the clearing, her staff in hand. The glow that had once emanated from it was dim, like embers slowly cooling after a great fire. Her body still ached from the strain of channeling the essence, but she remained upright, watching as warriors and Shamans worked side by side to clear the remnants of the shadow beasts and rebuild what had been lost.

Torin approached, his footsteps quiet but deliberate. He stopped beside her, crossing his arms as he followed her gaze. "They're already starting to look like a real alliance," he said, his voice low.

"They are," Aria replied, her voice tinged with a mixture of relief and exhaustion. "It's strange, isn't it? Seeing them work together after everything."

"It's because of you," Torin said simply. "You gave them something to fight for."

Aria shook her head, a faint smile tugging at her lips. "They gave themselves something to fight for. I just reminded them it was worth it."

Torin's lips quirked in a rare smile. "Modesty doesn't suit you."

Before she could respond, Kaela's voice rang out, cutting through the morning air. "Aria! Torin! You're not just going to stand there and brood all day, are you?"

Kaela strode toward them, her spear slung over her shoulder. Her grin was wide, though there was a faint shadow in her eyes—lingering grief for those who hadn't made it through the battle. "We've got a lot of work to do, and as much as I love watching you two look heroic, I could use a hand convincing Khoran not to put the supply tents next to the cookfires."

Aria raised an eyebrow. "Khoran? I thought he was done being difficult."

Kaela snorted. "He's Thornclaw. Difficult is in his blood."

Aria sighed, shaking her head. "I'll talk to him."

Torin chuckled. "Good luck. He's stubborn."

Kaela smirked. "Coming from you, that's saying something."

As Aria moved toward the center of the camp, she caught snippets of conversation from the warriors and Shamans around her. The tone was lighter than it had been in weeks, their words carrying a cautious hope. She passed a group of

Willowclaw healers tending to the injured, their hands glowing faintly with essence as they worked. One of them, a young woman with streaks of dirt on her face, looked up and smiled.

"Thank you," the healer said, her voice soft but sincere. "For everything."

Aria paused, her chest tightening. "It wasn't just me," she said. "We all fought for this."

The healer nodded, her gaze unwavering. "But you showed us how."

As Aria walked on, Torin caught up to her, his voice low. "You need to get better at accepting compliments."

"It's not about me," Aria said, her tone firm but not unkind. "It's about all of us."

"You can still let them thank you," Torin pointed out. "You've earned it."

Before she could argue, Khoran's gruff voice cut through the din. "I still think this setup is ridiculous," he said, glaring at Kaela as she approached with a smirk. "Supplies should be secured, not sitting out in the open like bait."

Kaela rolled her eyes. "They're not bait, you old grouch. They're accessible. Big difference."

Aria stepped between them, raising a hand. "Enough. Khoran, the supplies are fine where they are for now. If you have a better idea, talk to Seris. She's overseeing logistics."

Khoran grumbled but nodded, stalking off toward the supply tents. Kaela grinned, her eyes sparkling with amusement. "You've got a knack for this leadership thing."

Aria shook her head, though a faint smile played on her lips. "Barely."

Kaela clapped her on the shoulder. "More than barely. Now, if you'll excuse me, I've got warriors to organize. Try not to let Khoran stress you out too much."

As Kaela walked away, Torin turned to Aria, his expression softer now. "You're doing it, you know. Healing this place."

Aria met his gaze, the warmth of his words settling over her like a balm. "It's not just me," she said quietly. "It's all of us."

He nodded, his voice steady. "But it started with you."

The two of them stood in silence for a moment, watching as the tribes continued their work. The scars of the battle were still fresh, but the unity they had forged in the face of darkness was stronger than any wound. Together, they had saved Ilyria. And together, they would rebuild it.

The camp had grown quieter as the day waned, the sun dipping below the horizon in a blaze of orange and violet. Warriors and Shamans moved through the clearing with less urgency now, their tasks winding down as the reality of peace began to settle over them. The Astral Nexus, though still present in its quiet hum of dormant energy, no longer loomed as an ominous threat. It was simply there—a reminder of what they had overcome.

Aria sat on a low rock near the edge of the clearing, her staff resting against her shoulder. She gazed out at the horizon, her thoughts tangled between relief and uncertainty. The weight of the battle had lifted, but a new burden had replaced it: what came next. Her people would look to her now, not as a warrior or a leader in battle, but as the symbol of the peace they had fought so hard to win.

Torin's footsteps approached, soft and deliberate. She didn't need to turn to know it was him. His presence, steady and unwavering, was something she had grown to rely on more than she cared to admit.

"You're quiet," he said, his voice low as he settled beside her on the rock.

"I'm thinking," she replied, her tone light but introspective. "About everything that's happened. About what comes next."

Torin smirked faintly. "You mean what happens now that you're the Shattered Queen's heir? That's a lot of responsibility for one person."

Aria sighed, running her fingers along the smooth wood of her staff. "That's the problem. It's not just about me, but it feels like all of this is on my shoulders. What if I mess it up?"

Torin turned to her, his expression softening. "You won't."

"How can you be so sure?" she asked, her gaze still fixed on the horizon. "There's so much that can go wrong. The tribes are united now, but what if it doesn't last? What if the rifts reopen, or another Morvan rises? What if I'm not enough?"

"You've already proven you're enough," Torin said, his voice firm but gentle. "You brought them together when no one else could. You fought for them, not for glory or power, but because you believed in something bigger than yourself. That's why they'll follow you. That's why I'll follow you."

Aria turned to him then, her expression tinged with uncertainty. "You've always been by my side, Torin. Even when I doubted myself. Why?"

His dark eyes held hers, unflinching. "Because you're worth believing in. From the moment I saw you stand up to the Verdant Clans, I knew you were different. You don't just fight—you inspire. And you don't do it alone. That's what makes you strong."

She smiled faintly, though her voice was quiet. "You make it sound like I'm invincible."

"You're not," Torin said, a flicker of a grin crossing his face. "But you don't have to be. Invincible is overrated."

Aria laughed softly, shaking her head. "You're terrible at pep talks, you know."

"Maybe," Torin said, leaning back on his hands. "But I mean every word. You've earned their trust, Aria. You've earned mine."

Her chest tightened at the sincerity in his voice. "And what about you?" she asked, her tone softer now. "What happens to you after this? Will you stay?"

Torin's expression grew thoughtful, his gaze drifting to the distant campfires. "I've spent my life fighting for survival, for my clan, for Ilyria. I don't know what comes next. But wherever you go, I'll be there."

"Always the stoic protector," she teased, though her smile was tinged with gratitude.

"It's what I'm good at," he replied, his voice light. Then his tone softened, a rare vulnerability slipping through. "But it's more than that. I believe in you, Aria. Not just as a leader, or the Shattered Queen's heir, but as you. Whatever happens next, I'll stand by you."

Her smile faltered for a moment, replaced by something deeper, something unspoken. "Thank you," she said, her voice barely above a whisper.

They sat in silence for a while, the weight of the moment settling between them. It wasn't heavy, but it was significant, a quiet acknowledgment of everything they had shared and everything that was yet to come.

Finally, Torin stood, offering her his hand. "Come on," he said. "You've got a lot of people who want to see their queen."

Aria hesitated, then took his hand, letting him pull her to her feet. "I'm not a queen yet," she said, her tone half-teasing.

"Not officially," he replied, his smirk returning. "But you will be."

As they walked back toward the camp, side by side, Aria felt a flicker of something new—a sense of certainty, not just in her role, but in the people who stood with her. And at the heart of it all was Torin, her unshakable ally, her quiet strength, her steadfast companion. Together, they would face whatever came next. Together, they would shape Ilyria's future.

The glow of the Astral Nexus had dimmed, its once-swirling energy now calm, like a sleeping giant. The platform, fractured from the battle, felt solemn underfoot, a sacred space where the echoes of Ilyria's triumph lingered. Aria stood in the center, her staff faintly pulsing with essence. Before her, a shimmering portal hung in the air, its surface rippling like water caught in moonlight.

Torin was the first to speak, his voice low. "It's your way back, isn't it?"

Aria nodded slowly, her gaze fixed on the portal. "I think so. It feels… familiar, like it's calling me home."

Kaela appeared at the edge of the platform, her spear resting on her shoulder. "Well, that's convenient. Portal to your old life just opens up after you save the world? Doesn't seem suspicious at all."

Aria's lips twitched into a faint smile. "It's not suspicious. It's… a choice."

Kaela raised an eyebrow. "A choice, huh? Stay here and lead us stubborn fools, or go back to wherever it is you came from?"

"Something like that," Aria murmured.

Torin stepped closer, his expression unreadable. "And what do you want?"

Aria hesitated, her fingers brushing the smooth wood of her staff. "I don't know. This was never supposed to be my life. I didn't ask for any of this."

Kaela snorted. "Yeah, well, neither did the rest of us. Life doesn't exactly hand out what we ask for. It's more of a 'take what you're given and figure it out' kind of deal."

Aria glanced at her, the corner of her mouth lifting. "I'm starting to realize that."

Torin's voice softened. "You've already done more than anyone could have asked of you. If you want to go home, no one here would blame you."

"That's just it," Aria said, her voice tinged with frustration. "I don't know if I want to go home. I miss it—my family, my life. But after everything that's happened here, how could I just… leave?"

Kaela tilted her head, her sharp gaze meeting Aria's. "Maybe you should ask yourself this: what does home mean to you now?"

Aria blinked, the question settling over her like a weight. She turned back to the portal, its shimmering surface reflecting faint glimpses of her past—her quiet town, her family's smiling faces, the life she had left behind. But the image felt distant, almost like a dream she could barely remember.

Torin's voice broke through her thoughts. "You've changed, Aria. You're not the same person who fell into the Verdant Clans' camp that day."

She looked at him, her heart tightening. "I don't feel like the same person. But that doesn't make this any easier."

Torin's gaze held hers, steady and unwavering. "No, it doesn't. But the person you are now? She's capable of making this choice."

Kaela let out a sigh, gesturing to the portal. "Look, you've got the shiny door to your old life right there. If you want it, take it. But if you ask me, Ilyria needs you more."

"Kaela—" Aria began.

"No, let me finish," Kaela interrupted, pointing a finger at her. "You've done something no one else could. You brought us together, made us believe in something bigger than ourselves. If you walk away now, fine, but don't think for a second that this place will be the same without you."

Aria's throat tightened, the weight of their words pressing against her. She turned back to the portal, her thoughts a whirlwind. "I came here by accident," she said softly. "I didn't know anything about this place or its people. And now... I can't imagine leaving it behind."

Torin's voice was almost a whisper. "Then don't."

She looked at him, her eyes searching his. "It's not that simple."

"It is," he said. "Stay, and you'll have us. You'll have Ilyria. You'll have a purpose. Go, and... well, maybe you'll find something else. But you'll lose this. You'll lose what we've built together."

Aria's breath caught in her throat. She turned back to the portal one last time, watching as the images of her old life shimmered and faded, replaced by the faces of the people she had fought for—the tribes, the Shamans, her allies, and Torin.

Kaela clapped her hands together, breaking the silence. "So, what's it going to be, fearless leader?"

Aria closed her eyes, inhaling deeply. When she opened them again, her voice was steady, resolute. "I'm staying."

Kaela grinned, her sharp teeth flashing in the dim light. "Knew it."

Torin's expression softened, pride flickering in his dark eyes. "Good. Ilyria needs you."

Aria turned to him, her heart steady despite the weight of her decision. "I think I need Ilyria too."

The portal shimmered once more, then faded entirely, its light dissolving into the quiet hum of the Nexus. The platform fell silent, the finality of her choice settling over them.

Kaela swung her spear onto her shoulder. "Well, guess that's settled. Now let's get back to work. These tribes aren't going to lead themselves."

As Kaela strode away, Aria looked at Torin, her voice soft. "Thank you. For everything."

He nodded, his expression warm. "You don't have to thank me. I'm exactly where I need to be."

And for the first time since she arrived in Ilyria, so was she.

The Starstone Fortress, once cold and foreboding, now radiated a quiet reverence. Its ancient halls hummed with life as the tribes gathered to commemorate their unity and honor the one who had made it possible. The sun streamed through the high arched windows, casting brilliant patterns on the stone floor below. At the far end of the chamber, the prophecy's mural, long incomplete, had taken its final form.

Aria stood before it, her staff resting against the wall beside her. The vibrant depiction of her journey stretched across the stone, each detail alive with meaning. There she was, facing the shadows of Morvan, her staff alight with the essence of unity. The tribes flanked her in the mural, their weapons raised, their faces fierce and determined. At the center of it all was the Astral Nexus, its swirling energy no longer dark and foreboding but radiant and pure.

Torin stepped up beside her, his arms crossed as he studied the mural. "It's a good likeness," he said, his voice low. "Though they made you look a little taller."

Aria laughed softly, shaking her head. "I think they were being generous."

Kaela's voice echoed from behind them. "Generous? Please, that's exactly how I see you. Staff glowing, shadows scattering, looking like you could take down an army by yourself."

"Let's not inflate her ego," Torin said dryly, though a faint smile tugged at his lips.

Aria turned to Kaela, her expression warm. "You're not helping."

Kaela shrugged, leaning casually on her spear. "Hey, I'm just saying. If you're going to be immortalized in stone, might as well look good doing it."

The three of them shared a quiet laugh, the sound echoing softly in the vast chamber. Around them, the leaders of the tribes stood in clusters, their voices low as they discussed plans for the future. The scars of the battle were still fresh, but the unity forged in its aftermath was stronger than ever.

Seris, the braided-haired leader of the Willowclaw Clan, approached, her expression thoughtful as she regarded the mural. "It's strange," she said. "Seeing it all laid out like this. Like it's already a story we'll tell our children."

"It is," Aria said quietly. "But it's not just my story. It's all of ours."

Seris nodded, her gaze lingering on the image of the tribes standing together. "You gave us something to believe in again, Aria. That's not something we'll forget."

Khoran joined them then, his arms crossed as he studied the mural with his usual gruff expression. "It's impressive, I'll give you that. But don't think this means we're all best friends now. There's still work to do."

Aria smiled faintly. "I wouldn't expect anything less, Khoran."

Kaela smirked, nudging Khoran with her elbow. "Come on, admit it. You're a little impressed."

Khoran grumbled something under his breath, though there was no missing the faint flicker of pride in his eyes. "It's… decent," he muttered.

Aria turned back to the mural, her chest tightening with a mixture of pride and humility. "This isn't the end," she said softly. "It's a beginning. For all of us."

Torin glanced at her, his dark eyes steady. "You've given them a future, Aria. That's more than anyone could have asked for."

"It's not just about the future," she said, her voice firm. "It's about remembering what brought us here. Unity. Trust. That's what will keep Ilyria strong."

Kaela tilted her head, her sharp grin softening. "You really are the Shattered Queen reborn, aren't you?"

Aria shook her head. "I'm just me. And that's enough."

The room fell quiet as the tribes turned their attention to the mural, their gazes filled with awe and reverence. It wasn't just a work of art—it was a testament to their strength, their unity, and the courage it had taken to face the darkness together.

As the light from the setting sun cast the mural in a warm glow, Aria stepped back, her staff glowing faintly in her hand. Torin and Kaela stood beside her, their presence steady and reassuring.

"This is your legacy," Torin said quietly. "And theirs."

Aria nodded, her voice soft but resolute. "It's ours."

The tribes began to move, their voices rising as they discussed their plans to rebuild, to heal, to carry the unity they had forged into the days ahead. Aria watched them, her heart swelling with hope.

The mural was complete, but the story was far from over. It was the beginning of a new chapter for Ilyria, one written not by a single leader, but by the strength and unity of its people. And Aria, the Shattered Queen's heir, would stand with them every step of the way.

Epilogue
A World Rebuilt

The wind carried the scent of renewal, a mix of fresh rain and blooming wildflowers. Aria stood atop the edge of the rebuilt Temple of Seluna, its once-crumbled stones now polished and restored, each etched symbol glowing faintly with the essence that had bonded her to this world. The jungle stretched before her in vibrant hues of green and gold, alive and thriving, a far cry from the fractured chaos she had first encountered.

Her fingers brushed the pendant hanging around her neck—a shard of the relic that had brought her here. Its power no longer frightened her, though its weight was a constant reminder of everything she had endured. She let out a slow breath, her gaze fixed on the horizon where the sun dipped low, painting the sky in hues of fire and amethyst.

The sound of footsteps behind her was soft but deliberate. She didn't need to turn to know it was Torin.

"You should be resting," he said, his voice carrying a hint of disapproval, though the sharpness it once held was gone.

"I will," she replied, her tone lighter now. "I just needed a moment."

Torin stepped to her side, his presence as steadying as it had always been. He had traded his battle-worn armor for lighter garb, though his blade still rested at his hip—a habit she doubted he would ever abandon.

"The tribes are waiting," he said, his dark eyes scanning the jungle below. "The council won't start without you."

Aria smirked faintly. "Imagine that. Me, leading a council."

Torin turned his head slightly, the corner of his mouth lifting in what might have been a smile. "You've come a long way."

"So have you," she countered, glancing at him. "I don't think I ever thanked you. For staying. For believing in me, even when I didn't."

Torin's gaze lingered on her for a moment before he looked away, the faintest trace of a blush creeping into his cheeks. "You didn't give me much of a choice."

She laughed softly, the sound carrying over the temple walls. It was a rare, genuine laugh, unburdened by fear or doubt. For the first time, it felt earned.

They stood in silence for a while, the weight of the past months settling between them—not as a burden, but as a shared memory. The rifts were sealed now, the fractures in the land and the people mended through unity and sacrifice. The tribes, once divided by mistrust and old grudges, had come together under her guidance. They still had a long way to go, but the foundation of something stronger was there.

"What's next for you?" Torin asked finally, his tone casual, though the question held deeper meaning.

Aria tilted her head, considering. "I'm not sure," she admitted. "For so long, it was about surviving, about figuring out how to fix this world. Now that it's done… I don't know who I am without that fight."

"You're still Aria," Torin said simply. "The Shattered Queen. The historian who stumbled into a prophecy and decided to rewrite it."

"Rewrite it?" She raised an eyebrow, a teasing glint in her eyes. "You make it sound so dramatic."

"It is," he replied, his voice steady. "You didn't just follow the prophecy. You changed it. You made it yours."

Her smile softened, her fingers brushing the pendant again. "Maybe. But I didn't do it alone."

Torin nodded, his gaze fixed on the horizon. "No one ever does."

The sun dipped lower, casting long shadows across the jungle. Below, the tribes began to gather in the temple courtyard, their laughter and chatter rising like a chorus of hope. Aria watched them for a moment, her heart swelling with a mix of pride and bittersweet longing. This world had become her home, but a part of her would always ache for the one she left behind.

"Come on," she said, stepping back from the edge. "They're waiting for us."

Torin followed her without hesitation, his steps matching hers. As they descended the temple stairs, the crowd parted to let them through, their faces lighting up with reverence and gratitude. Children ran past, their laughter ringing out as they played games Aria didn't recognize but found herself smiling at anyway.

The council chamber was simple yet elegant, its centerpiece a long table carved from a single piece of ancient wood. Representatives from each tribe sat around it, their expressions serious but hopeful. As Aria entered, they rose to their feet in unison, bowing their heads.

"Shattered Queen," one of the elders said, his voice thick with emotion. "You honor us with your presence."

"Please," Aria said, lifting a hand. "Just Aria. I'm no queen. Not anymore."

The elder hesitated but nodded, his respect undiminished. "Aria, then. Shall we begin?"

She took her seat at the head of the table, her back straight and her hands steady. The discussions that followed were long and complex, filled with debates about resource sharing, border agreements, and rebuilding efforts. Yet through it all, there was a sense of unity, a shared determination to ensure that the mistakes of the past were not repeated.

As the council drew to a close, Aria leaned back in her chair, exhaustion tugging at her limbs. Torin stood nearby, his watchful gaze a constant reminder that she wasn't alone.

"You did well," he said quietly as the elders began to disperse.

"Did I?" she asked, her tone half-joking. "Sometimes I feel like I'm just making it up as I go."

"Welcome to leadership," Torin replied, his smirk returning.

She chuckled, shaking her head. "It's terrifying."

"And yet you keep going."

"Because someone has to," she said, echoing words he had once told her.

The night deepened as the villagers lit lanterns, their golden glow illuminating the temple courtyard. Music drifted through the air, and the people began to celebrate, their laughter and songs filling the space with life.

Aria watched from the edge of the gathering, her heart full but her thoughts distant. Torin joined her after a moment, his arms crossed as he surveyed the scene.

"You belong here," he said quietly.

She looked at him, her eyes soft. "Do I?"

He nodded. "More than you think."

For the first time, she allowed herself to believe him. This world, with all its challenges and beauty, had claimed her. And though the road ahead would be long, she was no longer afraid of it. She had found her place—not as a savior, but as someone who dared to hope, to rebuild, and to lead.

The Shattered Queen's story was over. But Aria's had just begun.

Milton Keynes UK
Ingram Content Group UK Ltd.
UKHW031438291124
451807UK00002B/219